W9-AAV-484

BABYMOUSE AND FRIENDS*

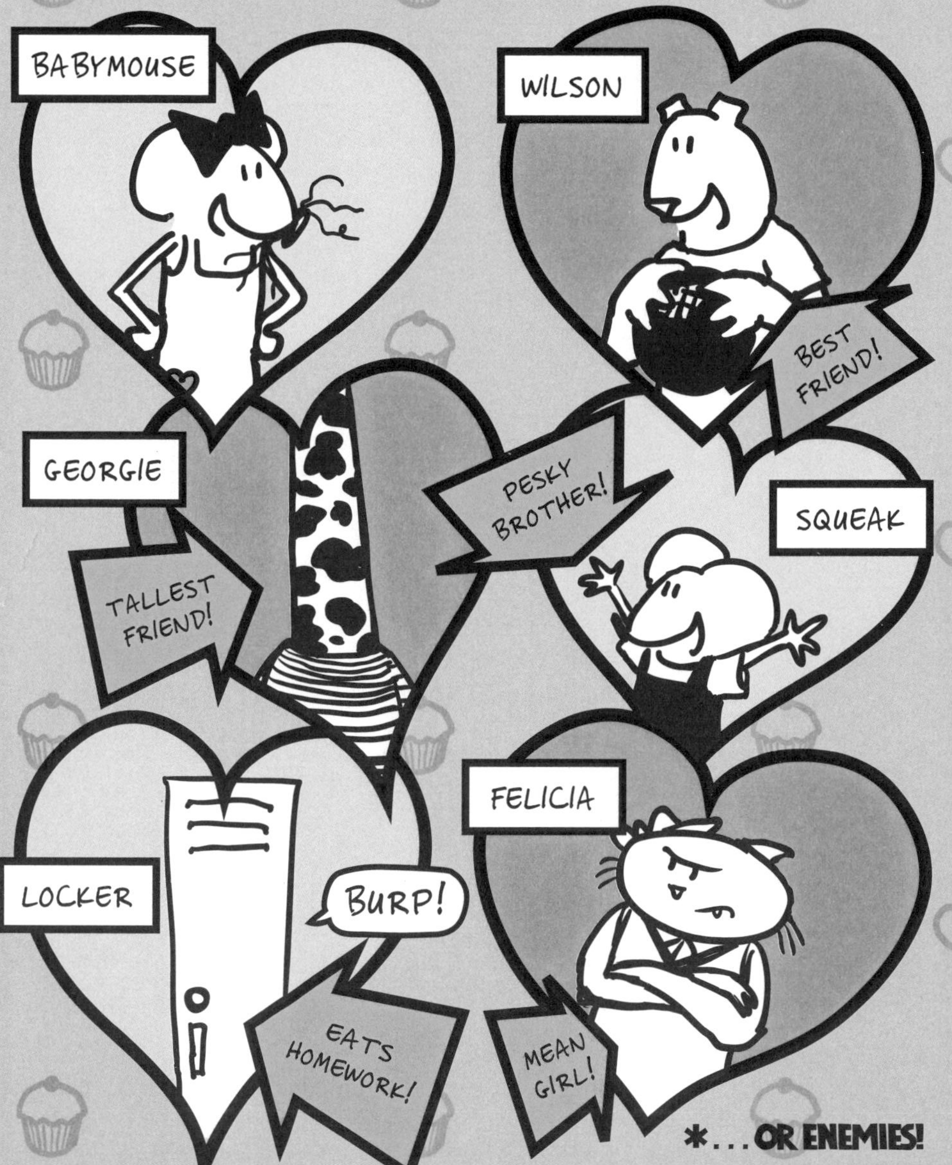
BABYMOUSE
WILSON
BEST FRIEND!
GEORGIE
TALLEST FRIEND!
PESKY BROTHER!
SQUEAK
LOCKER
BURP!
EATS HOMEWORK!
FELICIA
MEAN GIRL!

*. . . OR ENEMIES!

NO ONE CAN READ JUST ONE!

Be sure to read **ALL** the **BABYMOUSE** books:

#1 BABYMOUSE: Queen of the World!
#2 BABYMOUSE: Our Hero
#3 BABYMOUSE: Beach Babe
#4 BABYMOUSE: Rock Star
#5 BABYMOUSE: Heartbreaker
#6 Camp BABYMOUSE
#7 BABYMOUSE: Skater Girl
#8 BABYMOUSE: Puppy Love
#9 BABYMOUSE: Monster Mash
#10 BABYMOUSE: The Musical
#11 BABYMOUSE: Dragonslayer
#12 BABYMOUSE: Burns Rubber
#13 BABYMOUSE: Cupcake Tycoon
#14 BABYMOUSE: Mad Scientist
#15 A Very BABYMOUSE Christmas
#16 BABYMOUSE for President
#17 Extreme BABYMOUSE
#18 Happy Birthday, BABYMOUSE
#19 BABYMOUSE: Bad Babysitter
#20 BABYMOUSE Goes for the Gold

BABYMOUSE
QUEEN OF THE WORLD!

BY JENNIFER L. HOLM & MATTHEW HOLM

RANDOM HOUSE 🏠 NEW YORK

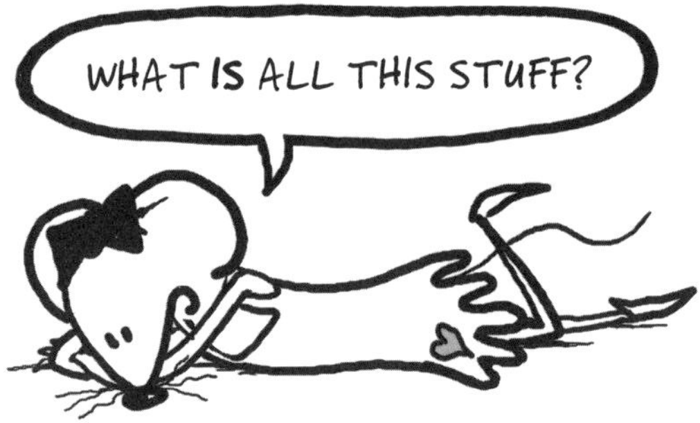
WHAT IS ALL THIS STUFF?

This is a work of fiction. Names, characters, places, and incidents either are the product of the authors' imagination or are used fictitiously. Any resemblance to actual persons, living or dead, events, or locales is entirely coincidental.

 Published in the United States by Random House Children's Books, a division of Penguin Random House LLC, New York.

Random House and the colophon are registered trademarks of Penguin Random House LLC.

Visit us on the Web!
randomhousekids.com
Babymouse.com

Educators and librarians, for a variety of teaching tools, visit us at
RHTeachersLibrarians.com

Library of Congress Cataloging-in-Publication Data
Holm, Jennifer L.
Babymouse : queen of the world! / Jennifer Holm and Matthew Holm
p. cm.
Summary: An imaginative mouse dreams of being queen of the world, but will settle for an invitation to the most popular girl's slumber party.
ISBN 978-0-375-83229-1 (trade) — ISBN 978-0-375-93229-8 (lib. bdg.) —
ISBN 978-0-307-97443-3 (ebook)
[1. Popularity—Fiction. 2. Imagination—Fiction. 3. Friendship—Fiction.
4. Mice—Fiction. 5. Animals—Fiction. 6. Cartoons and comics.]
I. Holm, Matthew. II. Title.
PN6727.H592B33 2005 741.5'973—dc22 2004051166

MANUFACTURED IN MALAYSIA 35 34 33 32 31 30 29 28 27 26 25 24 23 22

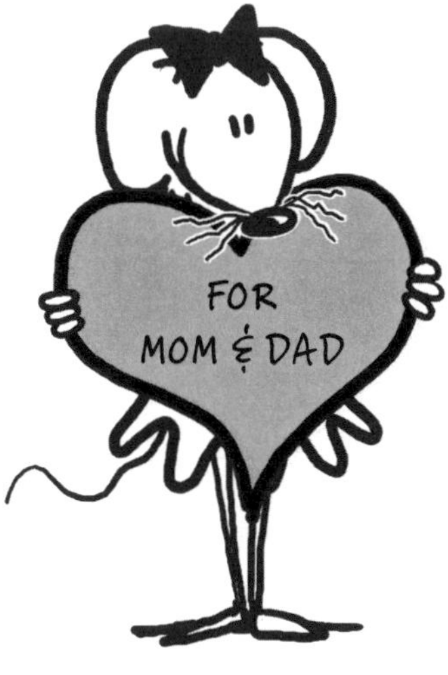
FOR
MOM & DAD

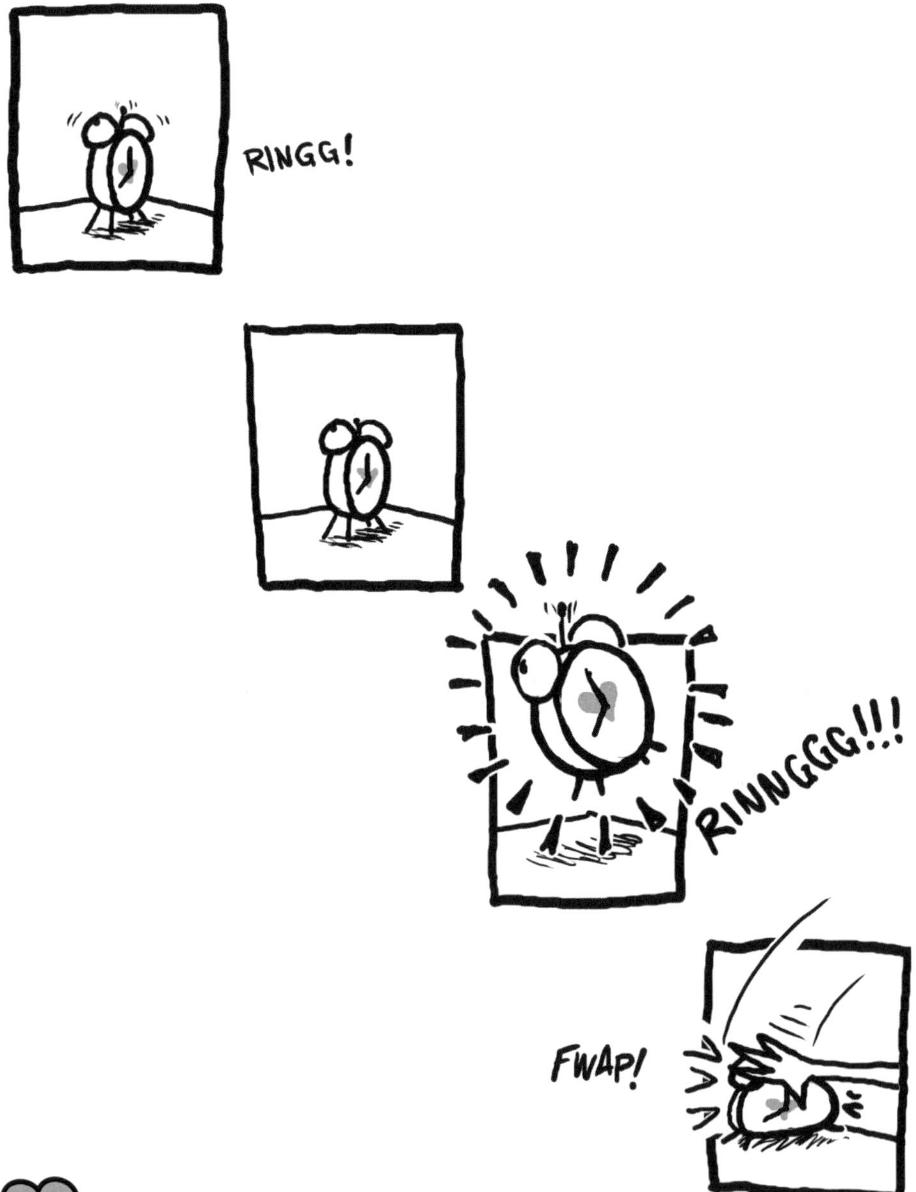
RINGG!
RINNGGG!!!
FWAP!

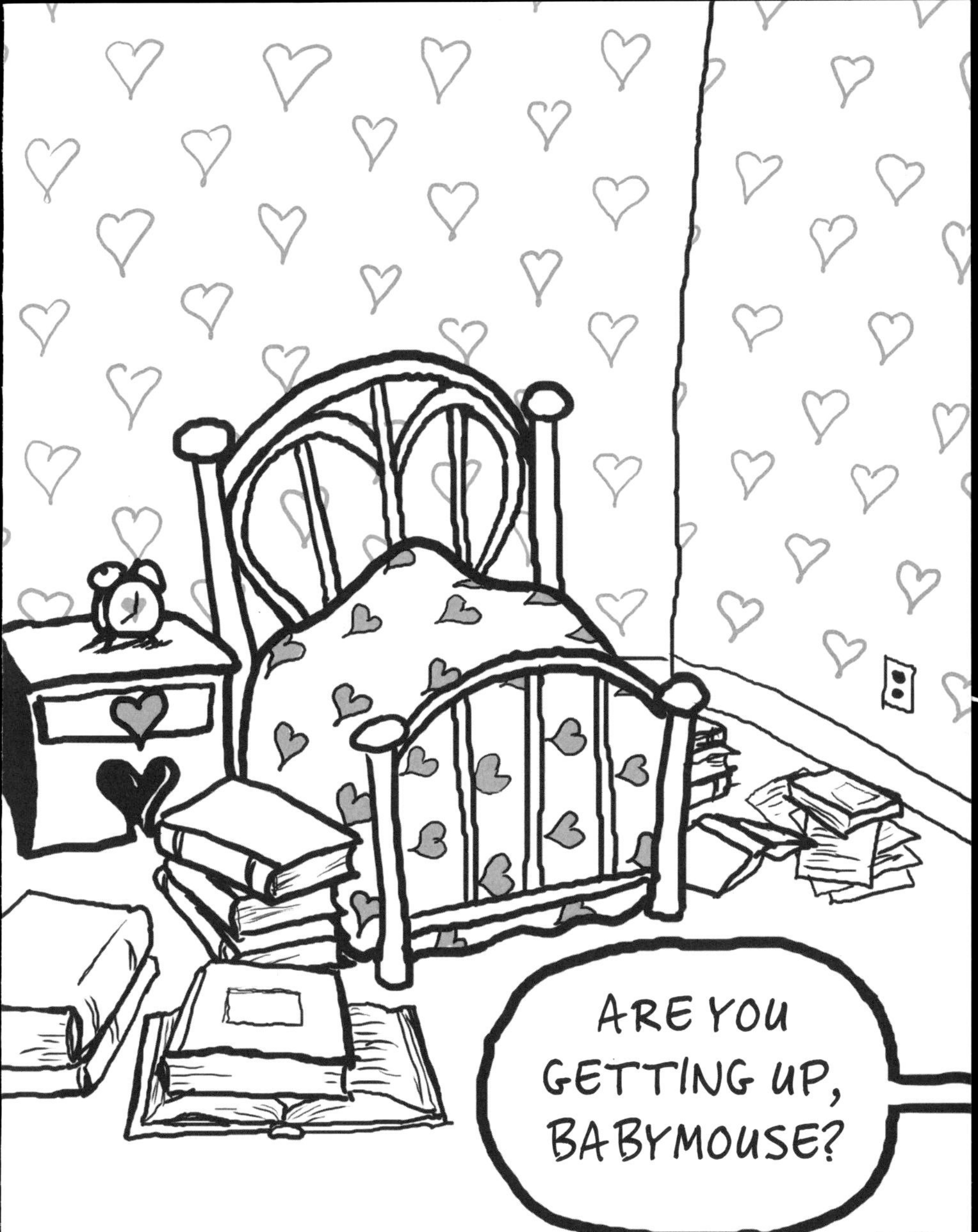
ARE YOU GETTING UP, BABYMOUSE?

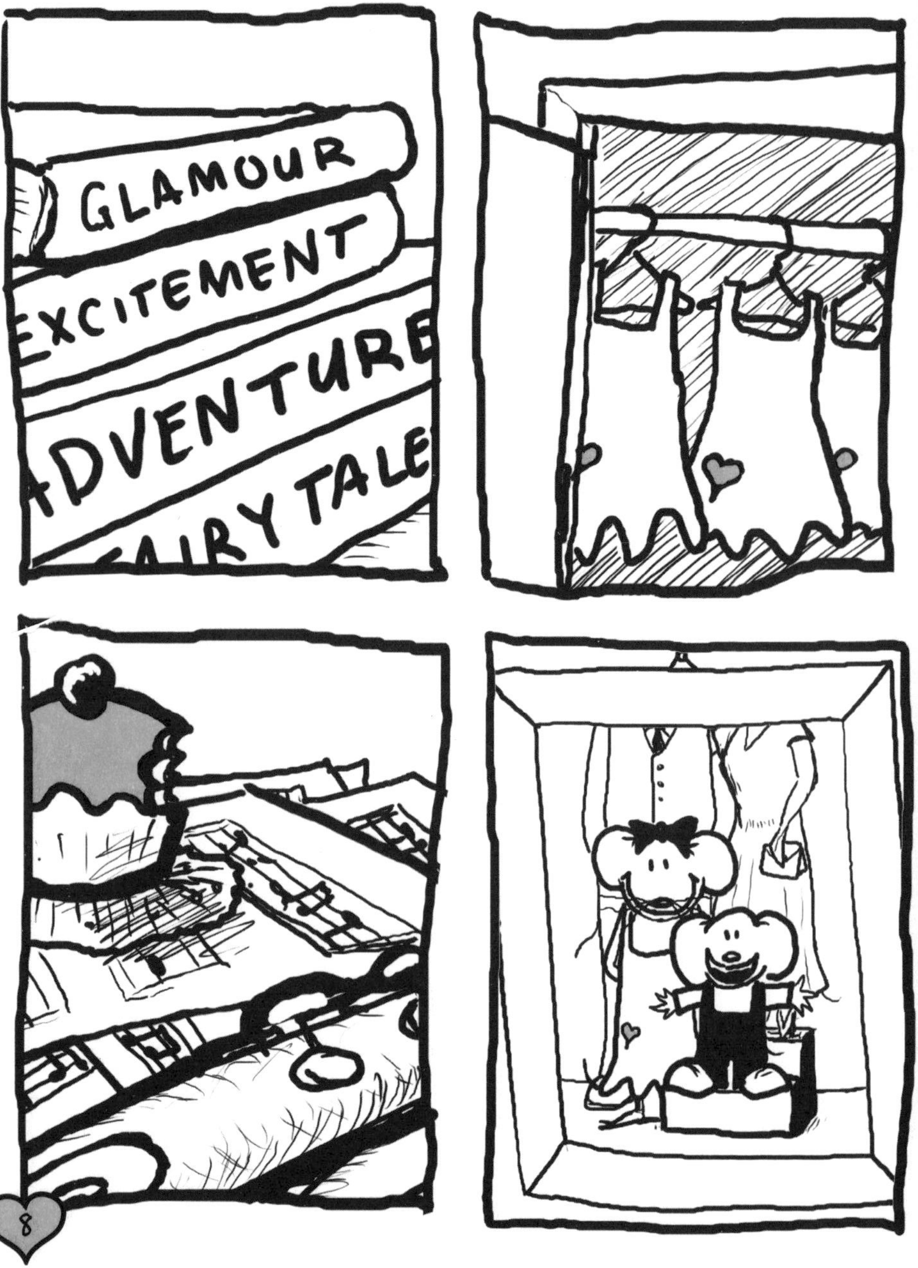
GLAMOUR
EXCITEMENT
DVENTURE
AIRY TALE

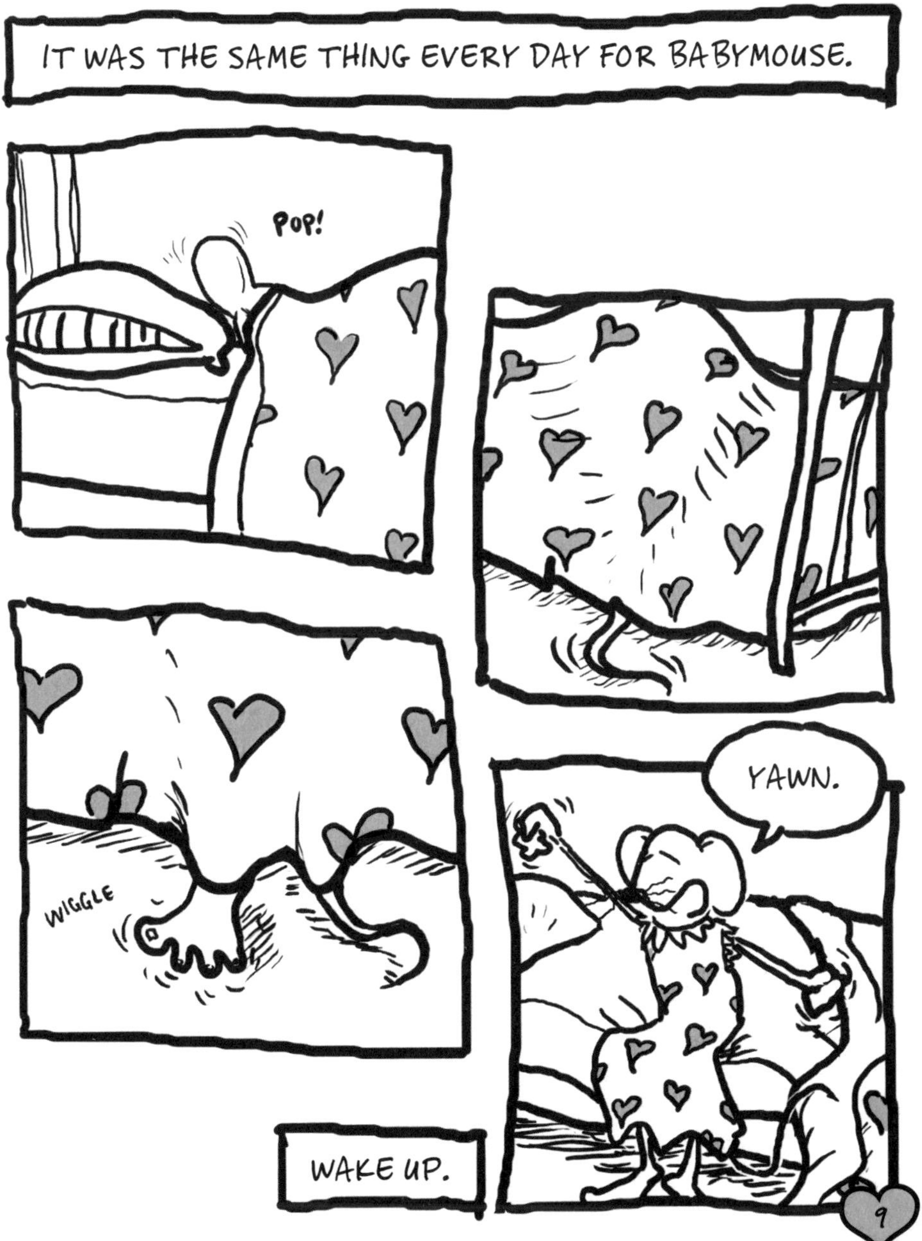
IT WAS THE SAME THING EVERY DAY FOR BABYMOUSE.
POP!
WIGGLE
WAKE UP.
YAWN.

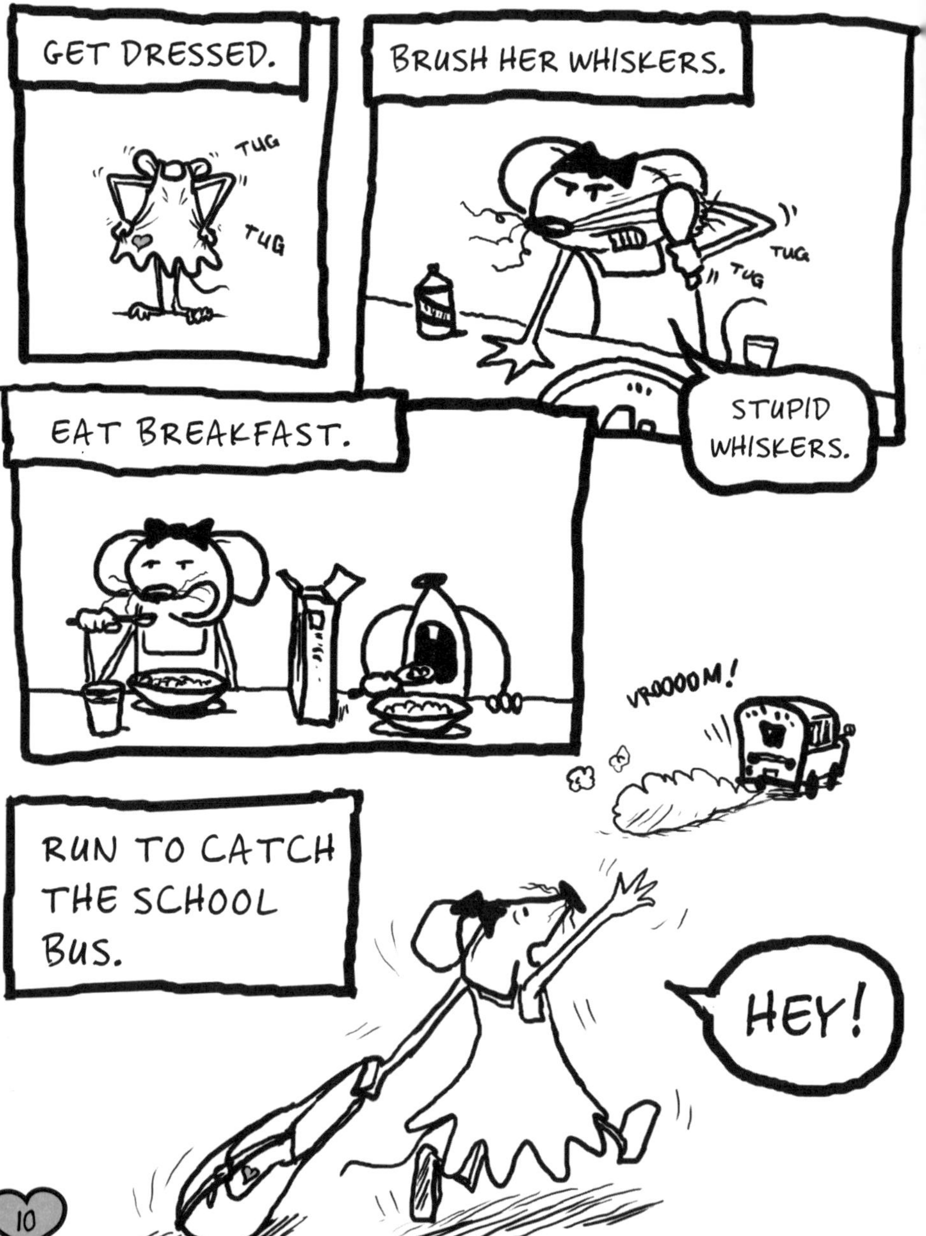
GET DRESSED.
TUG
TUG
BRUSH HER WHISKERS.
TUG
TUG
STUPID WHISKERS.
EAT BREAKFAST.
VROOOOOM!
RUN TO CATCH THE SCHOOL BUS.
HEY!

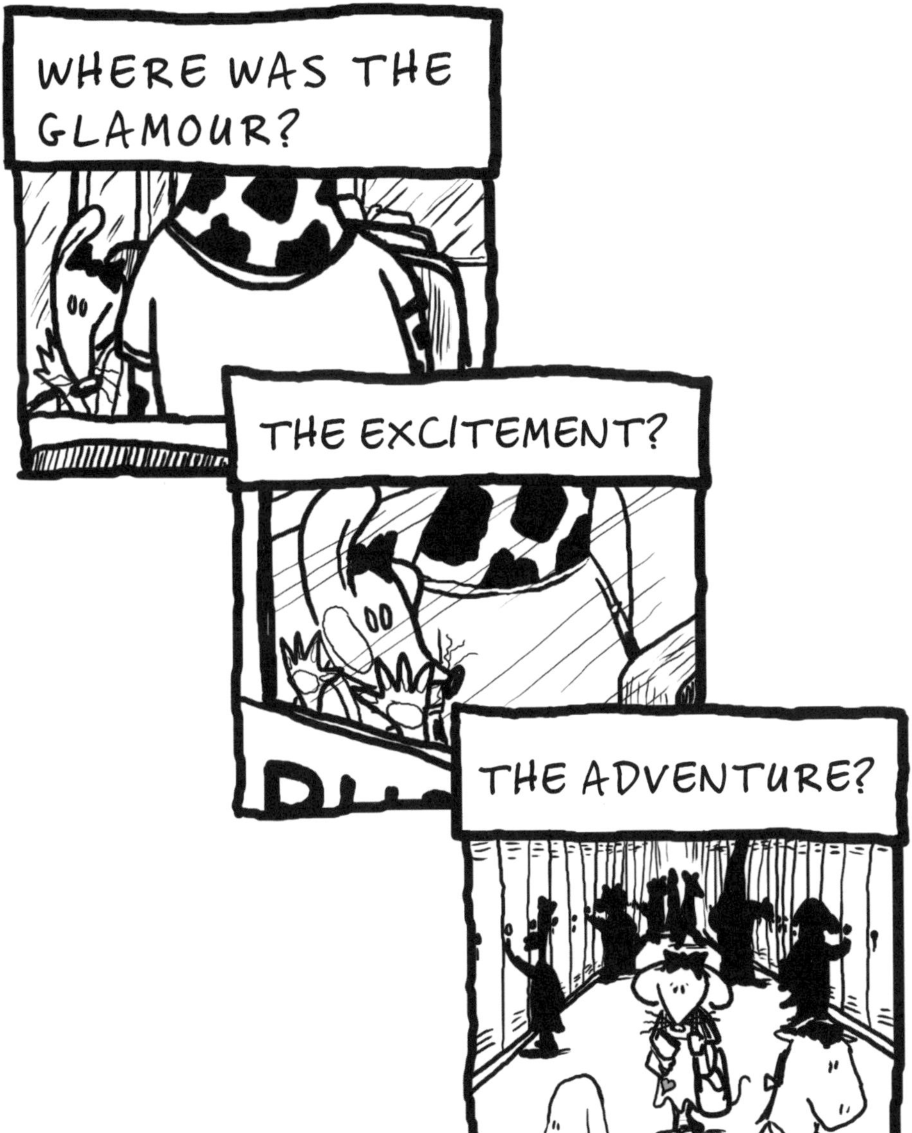
WHERE WAS THE GLAMOUR?
THE EXCITEMENT?
THE ADVENTURE?

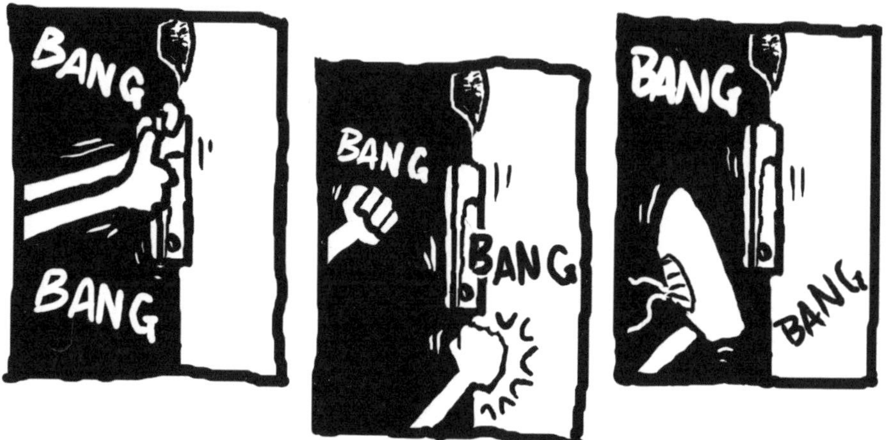
BANG
BANG
BANG
BANG
BANG
BANG

ALL BABYMOUSE HAD WAS AN OVERDUE LIBRARY BOOK AND A LOCKER THAT STUCK.

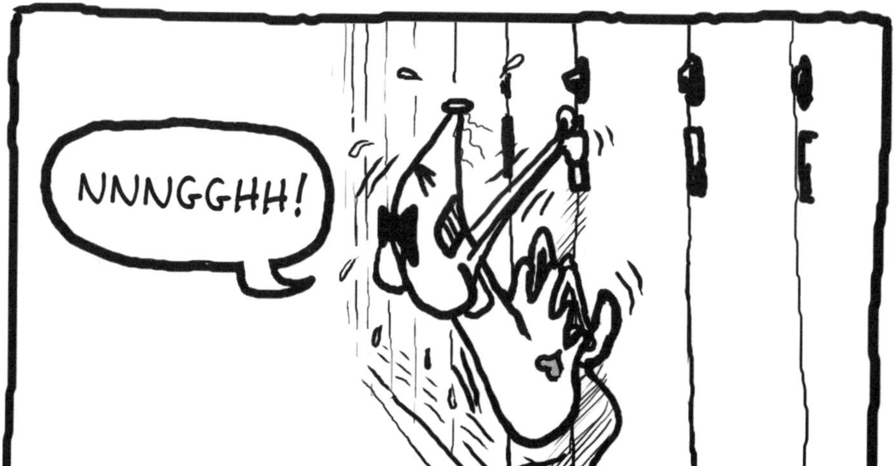
NNNGGHH!

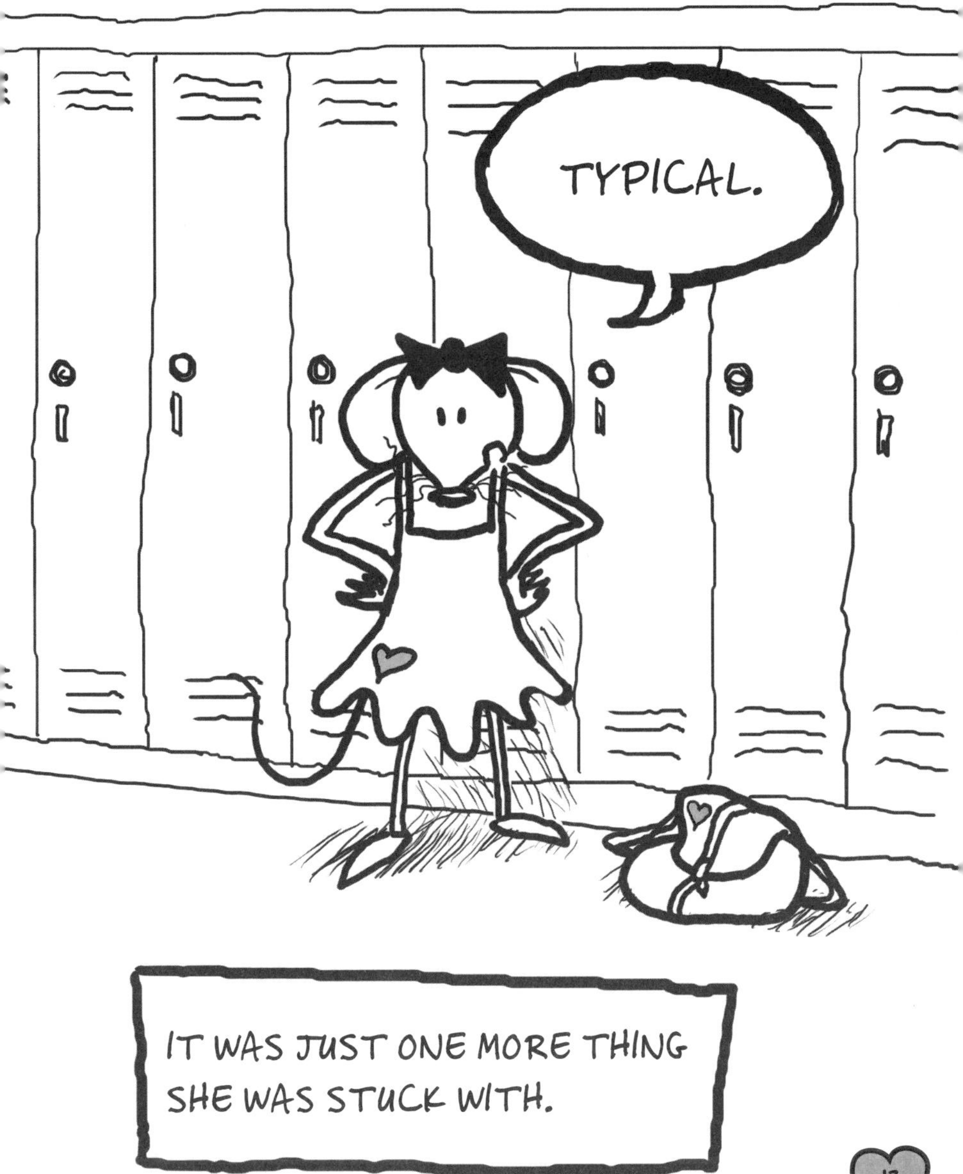
TYPICAL.
IT WAS JUST ONE MORE THING SHE WAS STUCK WITH.

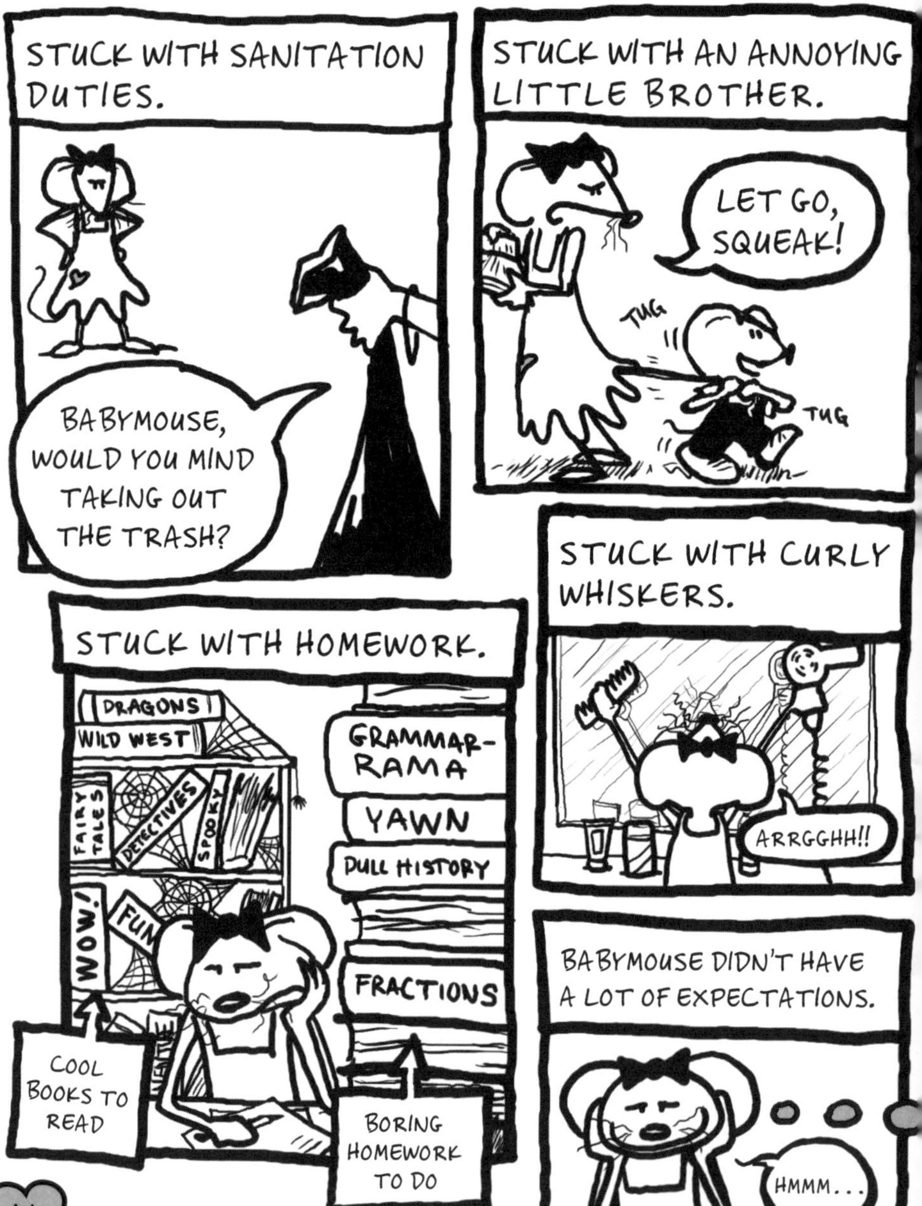
STUCK WITH SANITATION DUTIES.
BABYMOUSE, WOULD YOU MIND TAKING OUT THE TRASH?
STUCK WITH AN ANNOYING LITTLE BROTHER.
LET GO, SQUEAK!
TUG
TUG
STUCK WITH HOMEWORK.
DRAGONS
WILD WEST
FAIRY TALES
DETECTIVES
SPOOKY
WOW!
FUN
GRAMMAR-RAMA
YAWN
DULL HISTORY
FRACTIONS
COOL BOOKS TO READ
BORING HOMEWORK TO DO
STUCK WITH CURLY WHISKERS.
ARRGGHH!!
BABYMOUSE DIDN'T HAVE A LOT OF EXPECTATIONS.
HMMM...

WELL, MAYBE JUST A FEW.
TIARA!
STRAIGHT WHISKERS!
ICE CREAM FOR LUNCH!
NO HOMEWORK!
QUEEN OF THE WORLD!

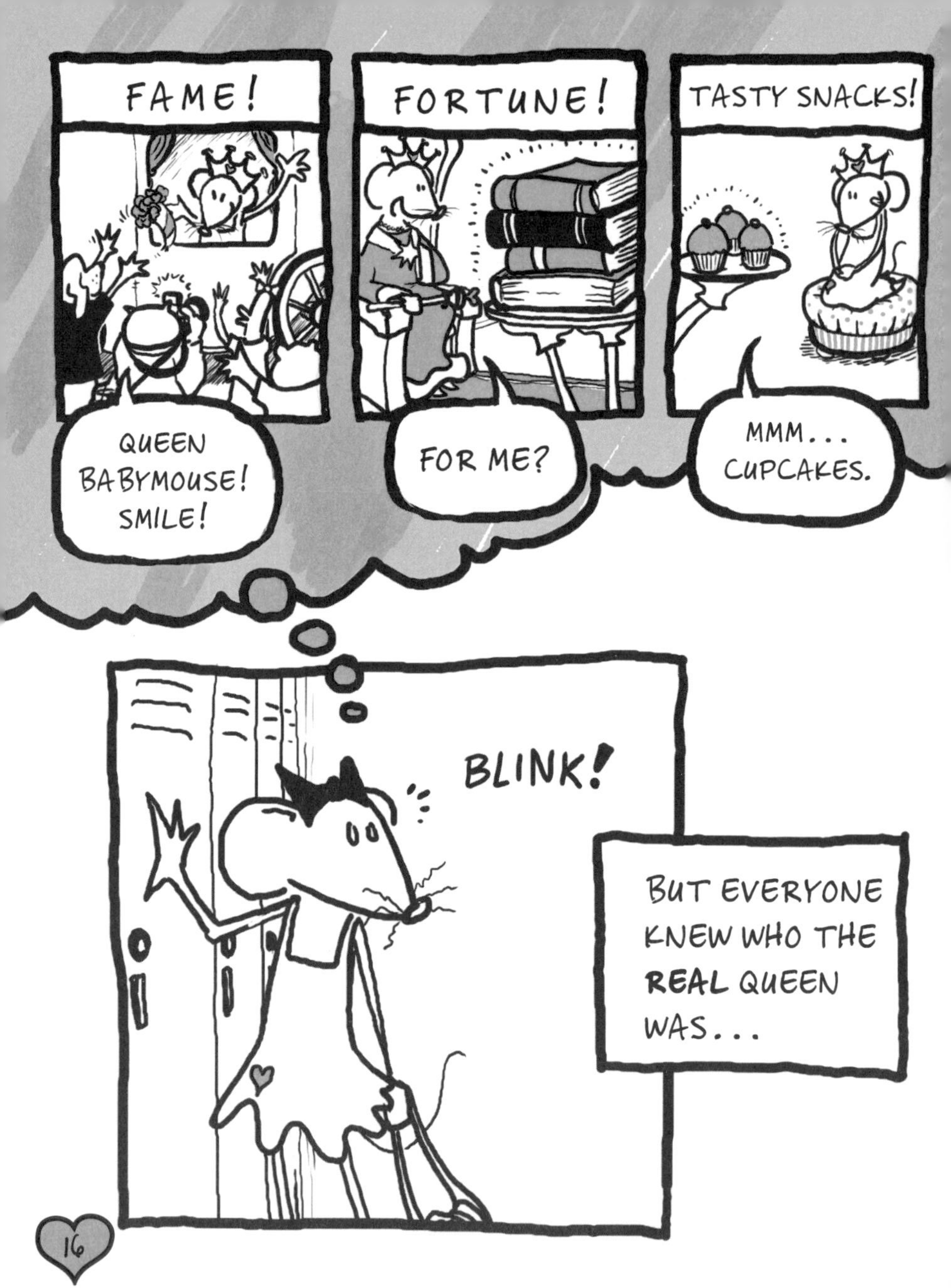
FAME!
QUEEN BABYMOUSE! SMILE!
FORTUNE!
FOR ME?
TASTY SNACKS!
MMM... CUPCAKES.
BLINK!
BUT EVERYONE KNEW WHO THE **REAL** QUEEN WAS...

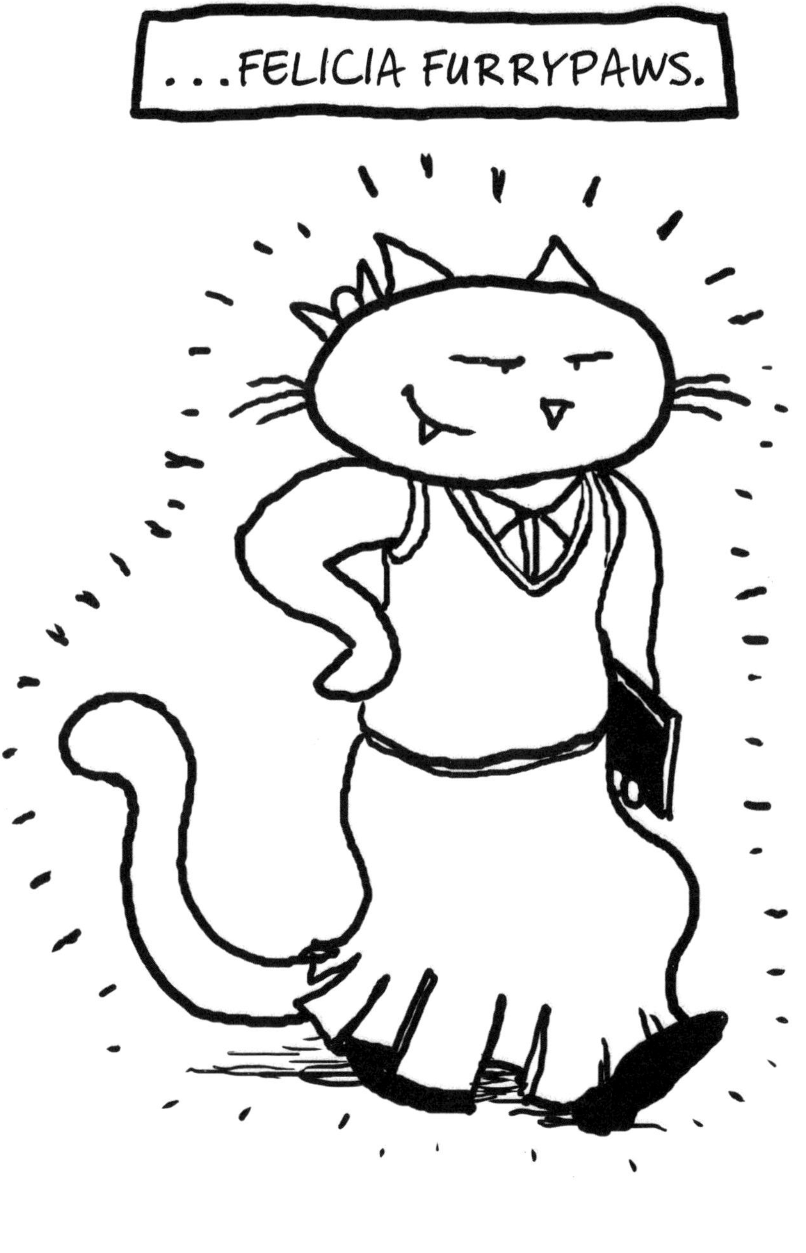
...FELICIA FURRYPAWS.

, HI THERE, FELICIA, HOW ARE YOU TODAY? I HEARD W
VI   I FOR LUNCH TODAY. ISN'T THAT J
EA   G'S BETTER THAN THAT MEAT.
HE   E. YUCK! I WONDER IF IT EVEN HAS
AT   NALLY, I DON'T REALLY LIKE ANY
AT   RD "LOAF" IN IT. WELL, EXCEPT BR
OU   COUNT? I GUESS NOT. OH—AND G
AT   HE NEATEST BOOK, ABOUT THIS
O   A WIZARD AND GETS TO GO TO
OL   OOL. ISN'T THAT COOL? I WISH WE W
A   OL. THEN WE COULD LEARN TO DO M
D   STUFF INSTEAD OF HAVING TO LE
OU   CTIONS. FELICIA, WH   OU LIKE

OKAY...
BE COOL...

18

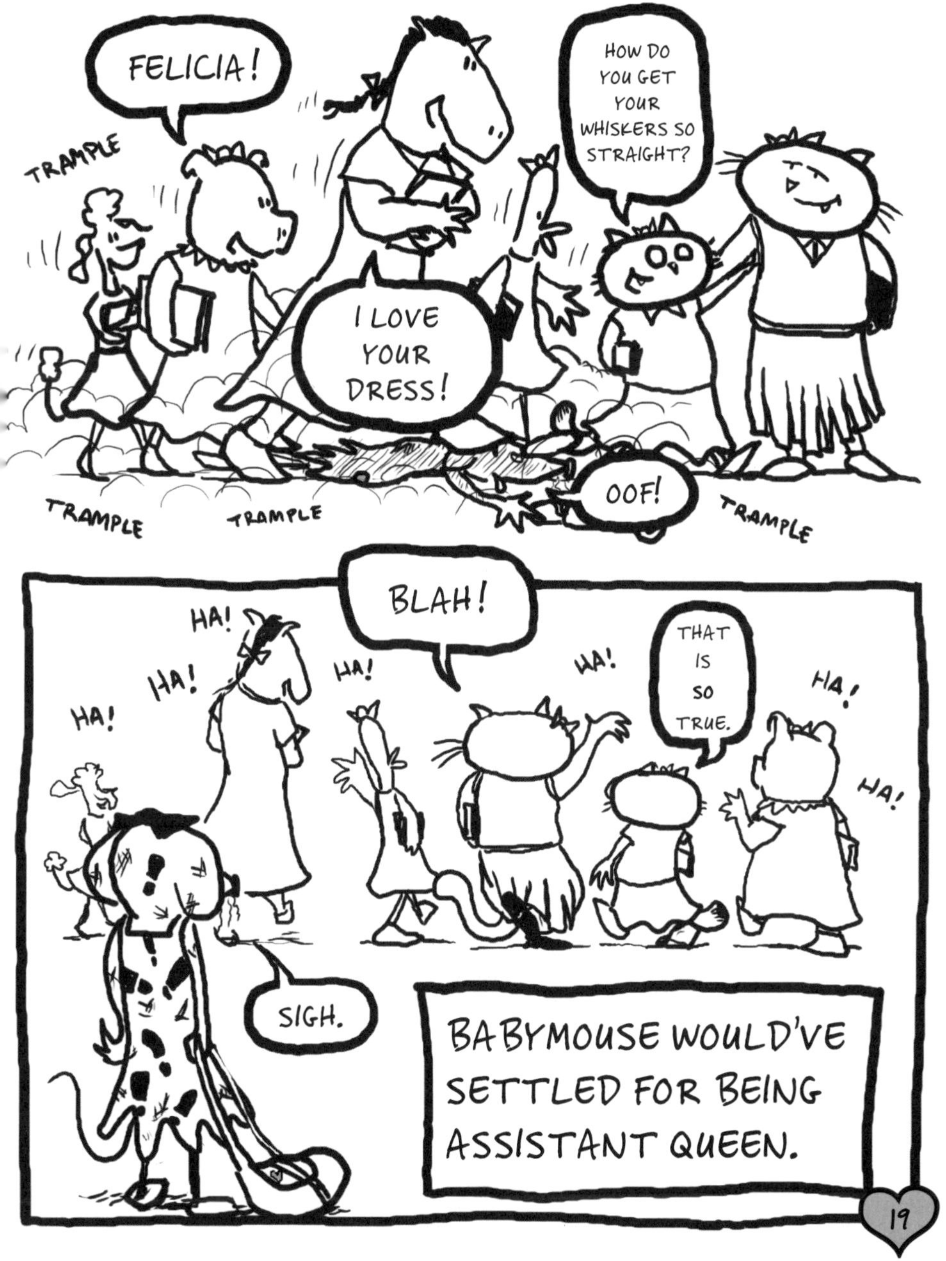

FELICIA!
TRAMPLE
HOW DO YOU GET YOUR WHISKERS SO STRAIGHT?
I LOVE YOUR DRESS!
TRAMPLE
TRAMPLE
OOF!
TRAMPLE
BLAH!
HA!
HA!
HA!
HA!
HA!
THAT IS SO TRUE.
HA!
HA!
SIGH.
BABYMOUSE WOULD'VE SETTLED FOR BEING ASSISTANT QUEEN.

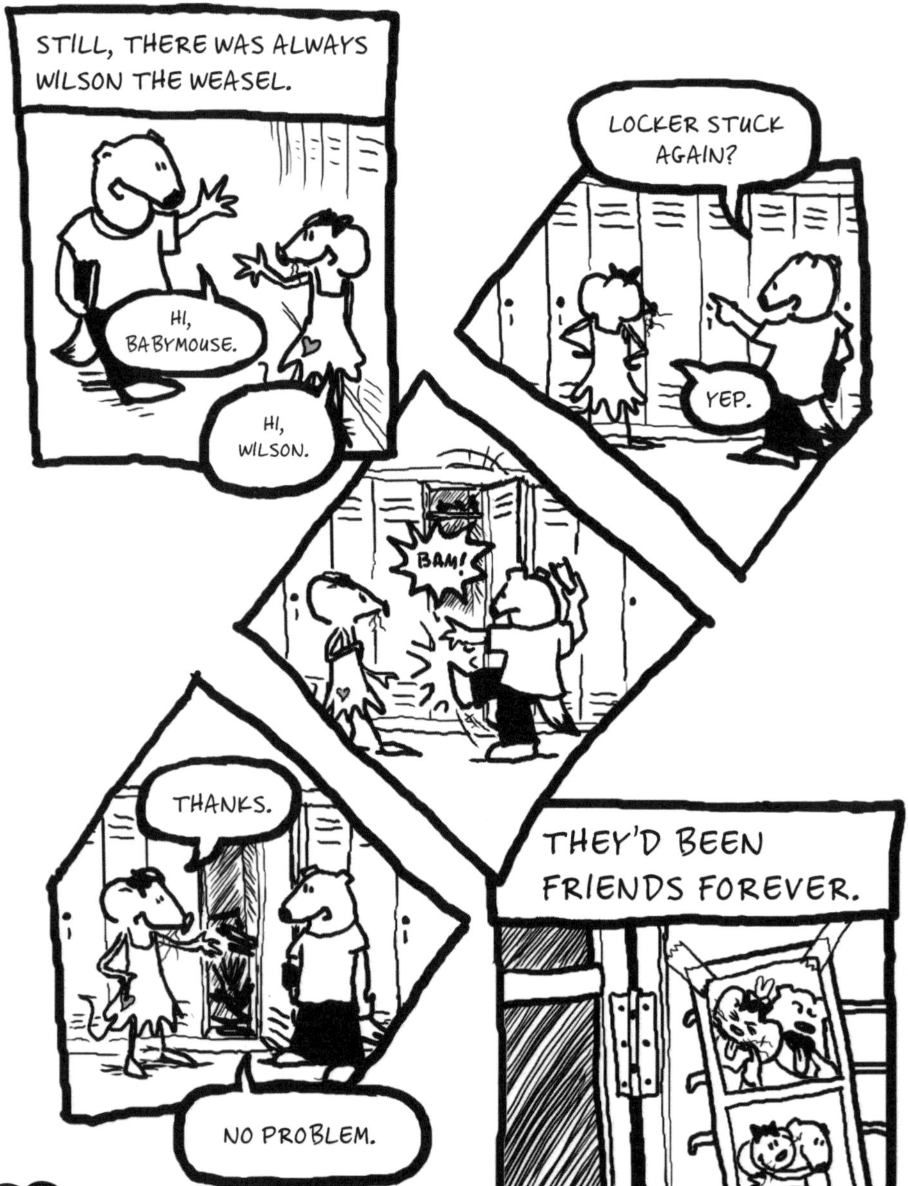
STILL, THERE WAS ALWAYS WILSON THE WEASEL.
HI, BABYMOUSE.
HI, WILSON.
LOCKER STUCK AGAIN?
YEP.
BAM!
THANKS.
NO PROBLEM.
THEY'D BEEN FRIENDS FOREVER.

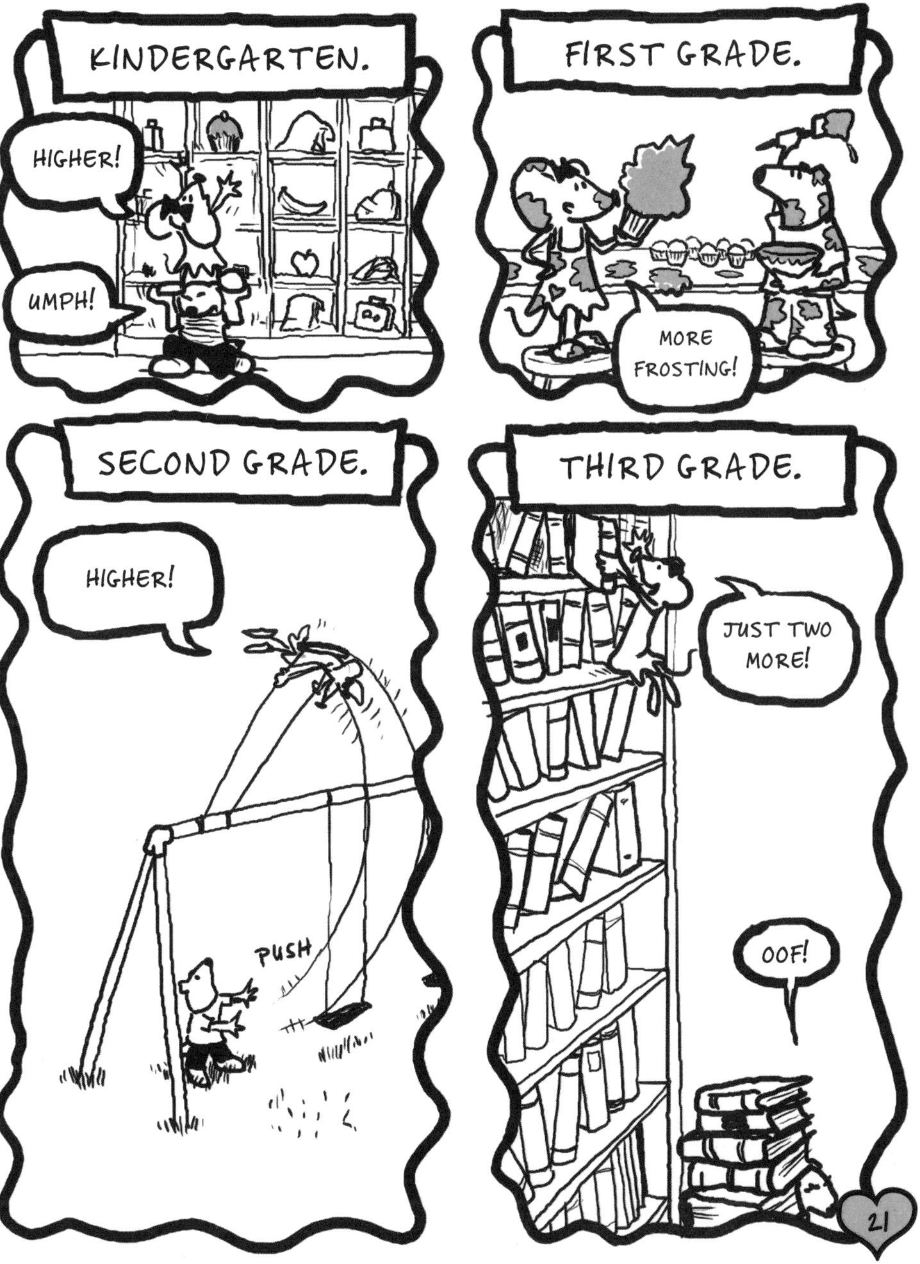
KINDERGARTEN.
HIGHER!
UMPH!
FIRST GRADE.
MORE FROSTING!
SECOND GRADE.
HIGHER!
PUSH
THIRD GRADE.
JUST TWO MORE!
OOF!

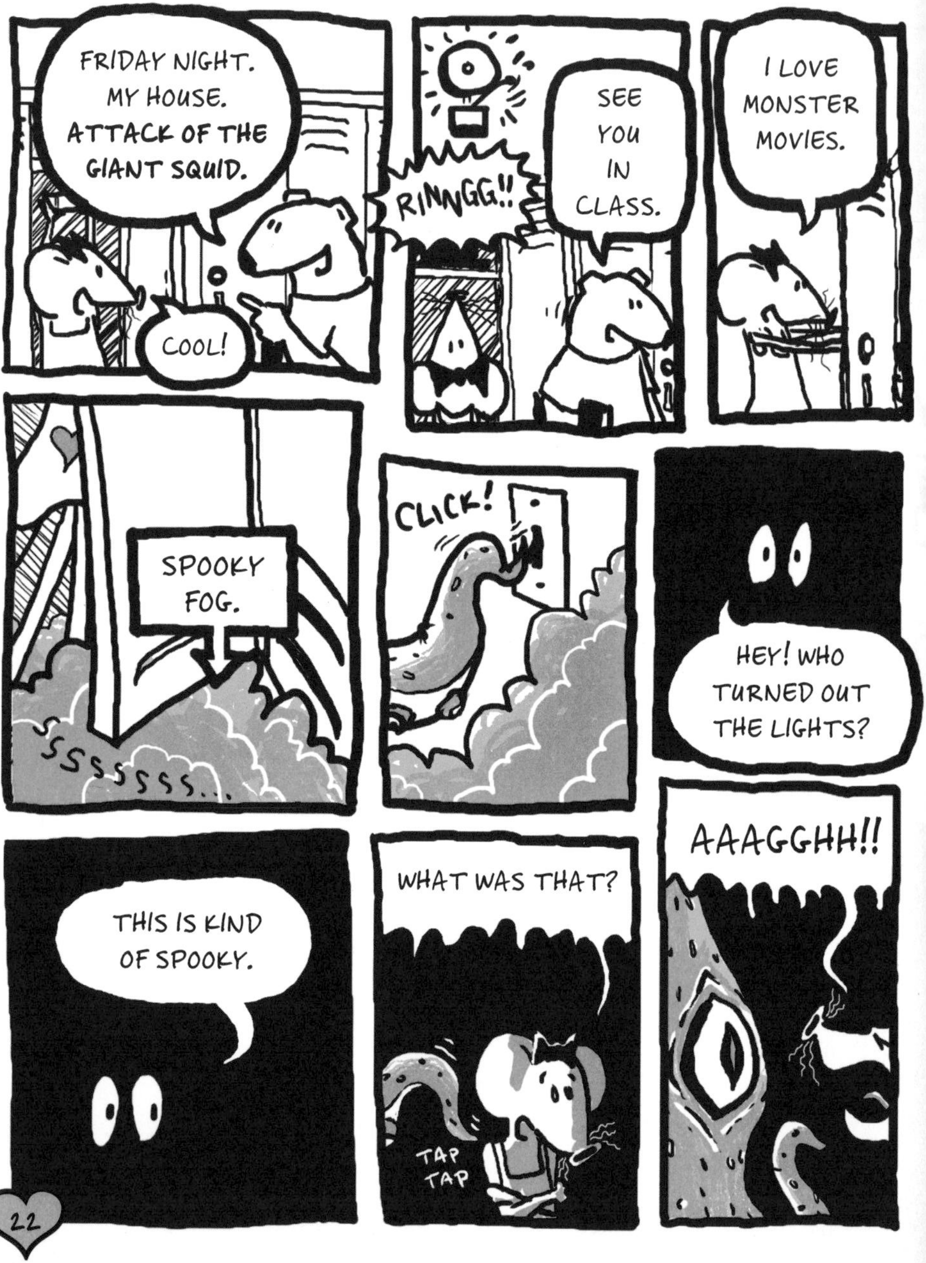

FRIDAY NIGHT. MY HOUSE. ATTACK OF THE GIANT SQUID.
COOL!
RINNGG!!
SEE YOU IN CLASS.
I LOVE MONSTER MOVIES.
SPOOKY FOG.
SSSSSSSS...
CLICK!
HEY! WHO TURNED OUT THE LIGHTS?
THIS IS KIND OF SPOOKY.
WHAT WAS THAT?
TAP TAP
AAAGGHH!!

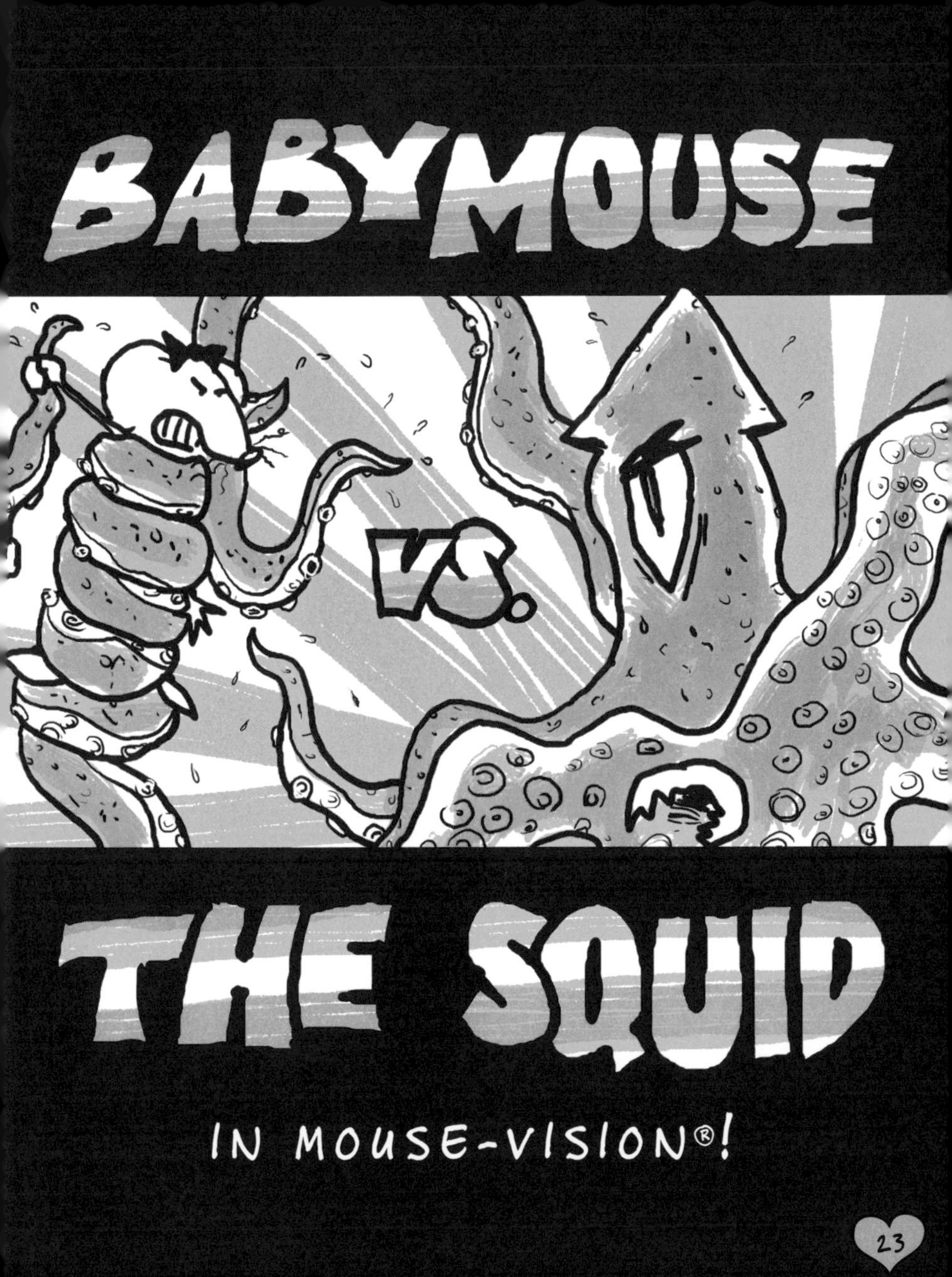
BABYMOUSE
VS.
THE SQUID
IN MOUSE-VISION®!

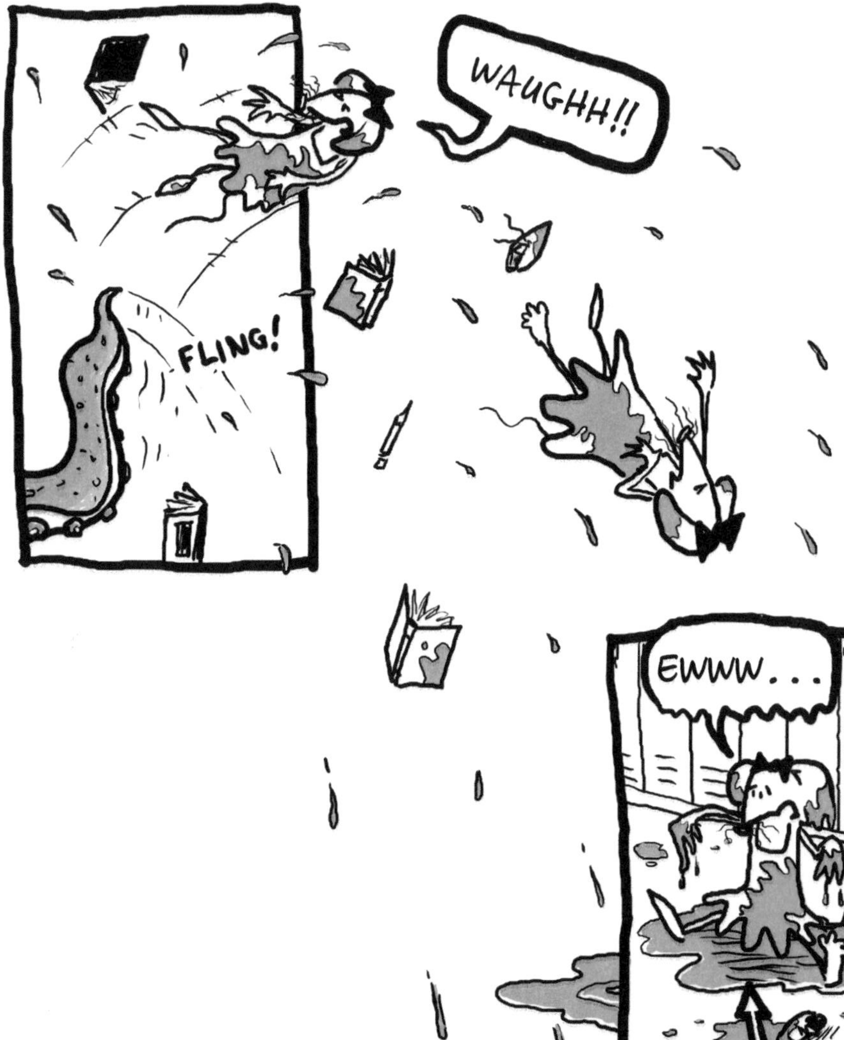

WAUGHH!!
FLING!
EWWW...
SQUID SLIME

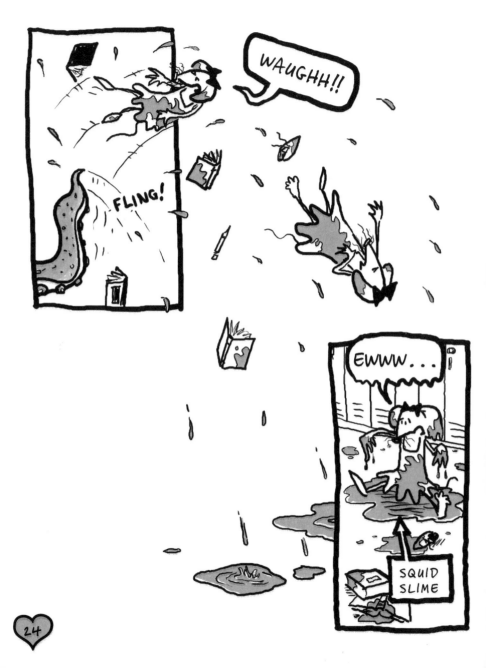

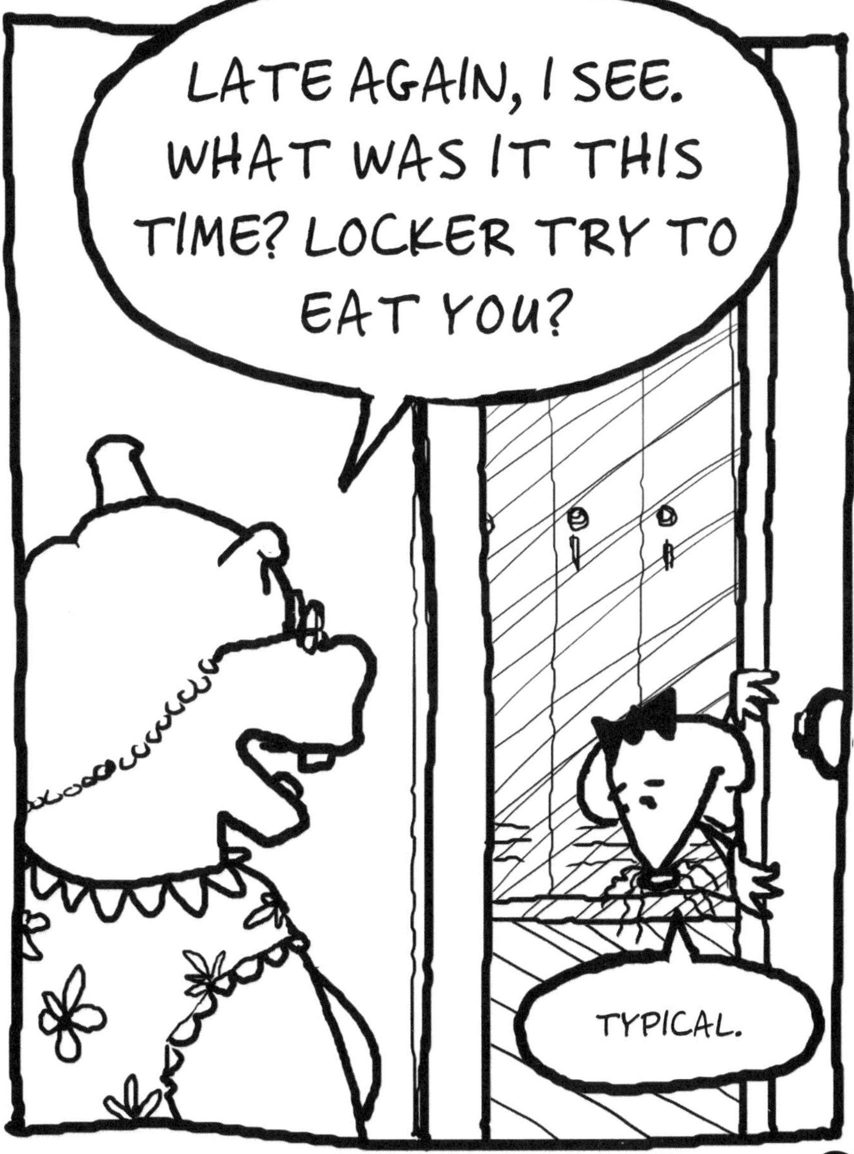
LATE AGAIN, I SEE. WHAT WAS IT THIS TIME? LOCKER TRY TO EAT YOU?
TYPICAL.

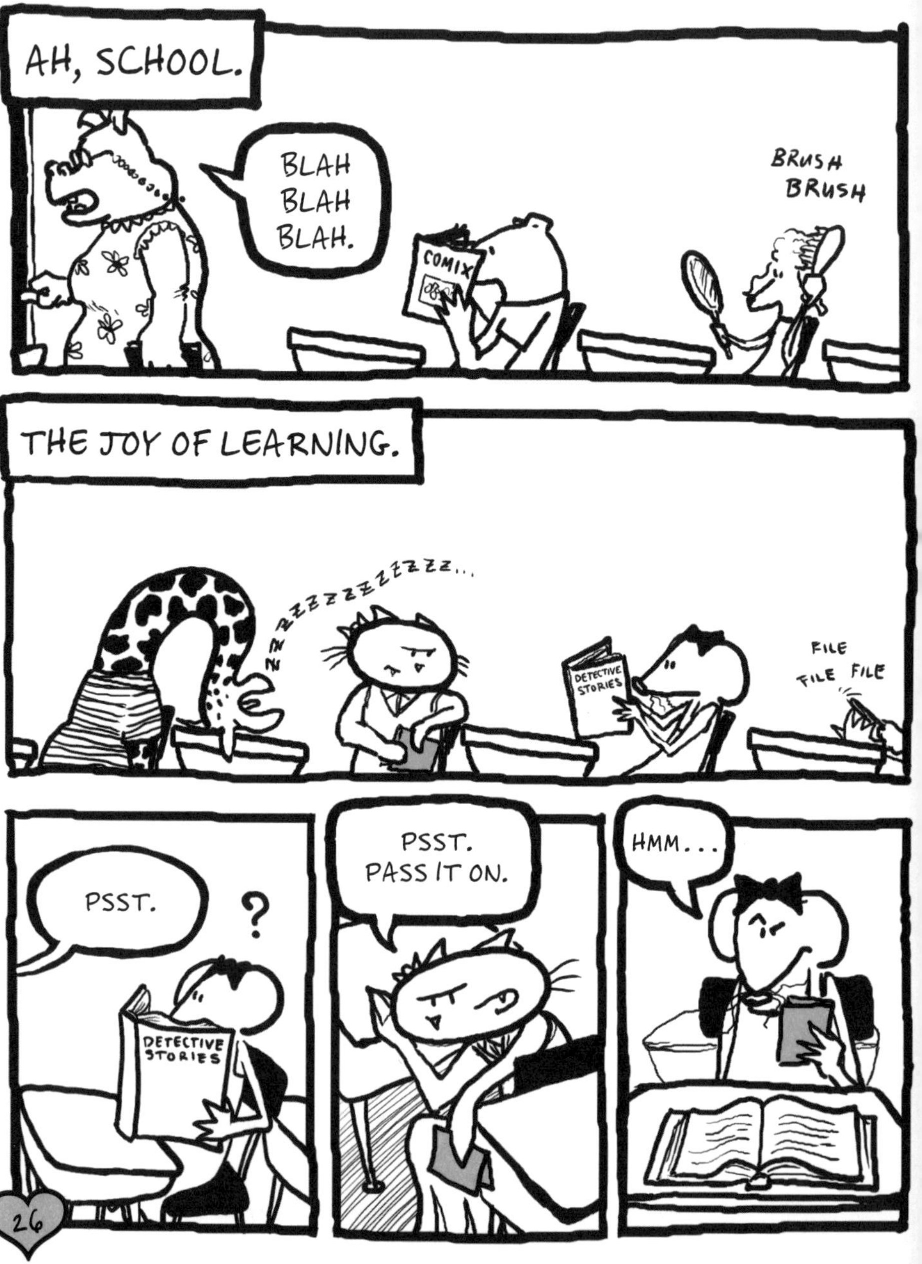
AH, SCHOOL.
BLAH BLAH BLAH.
COMIX
BRUSH BRUSH
THE JOY OF LEARNING.
ZZZZZZZZZZZZZZZZZ...
DETECTIVE STORIES
FILE FILE FILE
PSST.
?
DETECTIVE STORIES
PSST. PASS IT ON.
HMM...

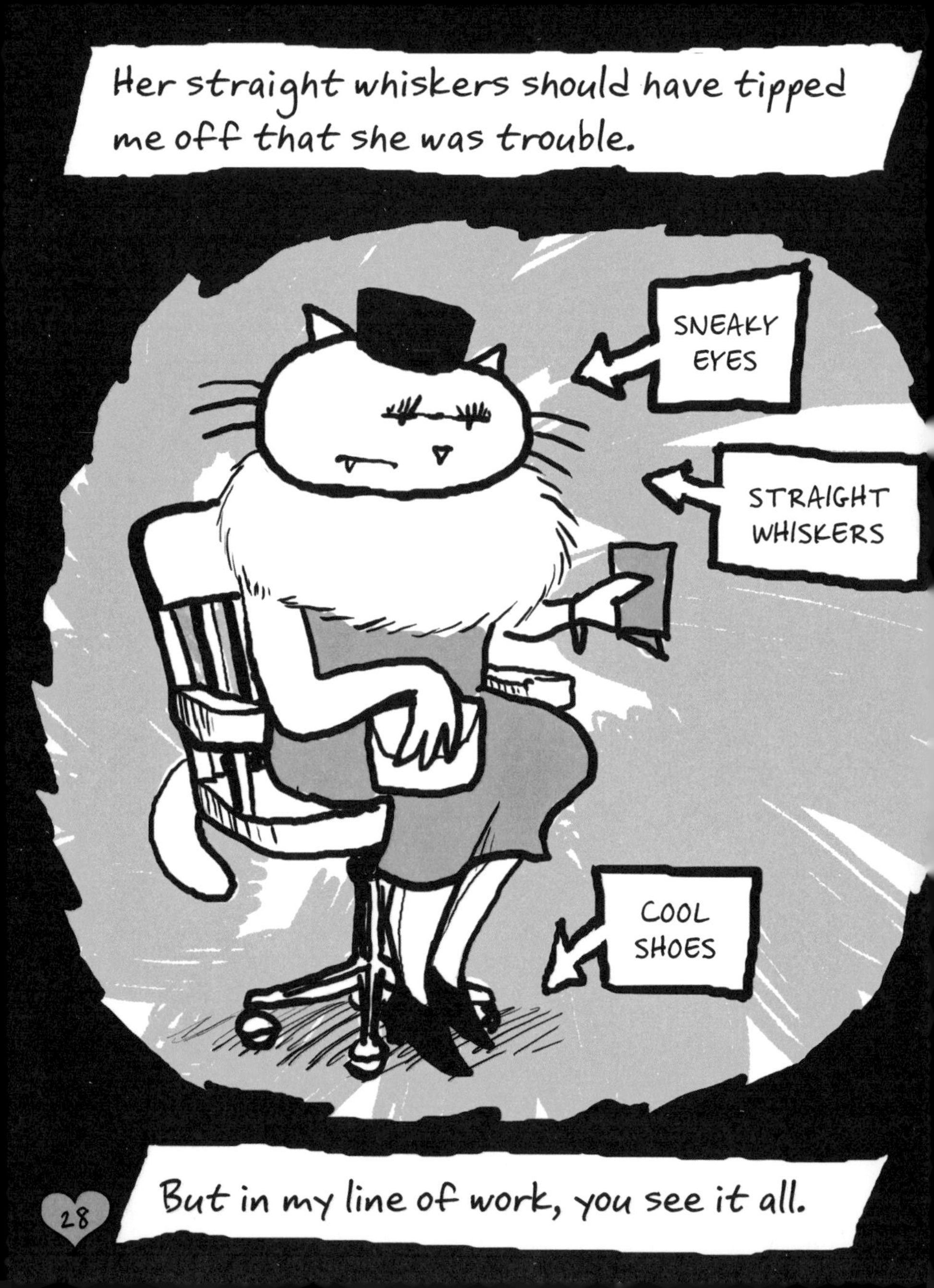
Her straight whiskers should have tipped me off that she was trouble.
SNEAKY EYES
STRAIGHT WHISKERS
COOL SHOES
But in my line of work, you see it all.

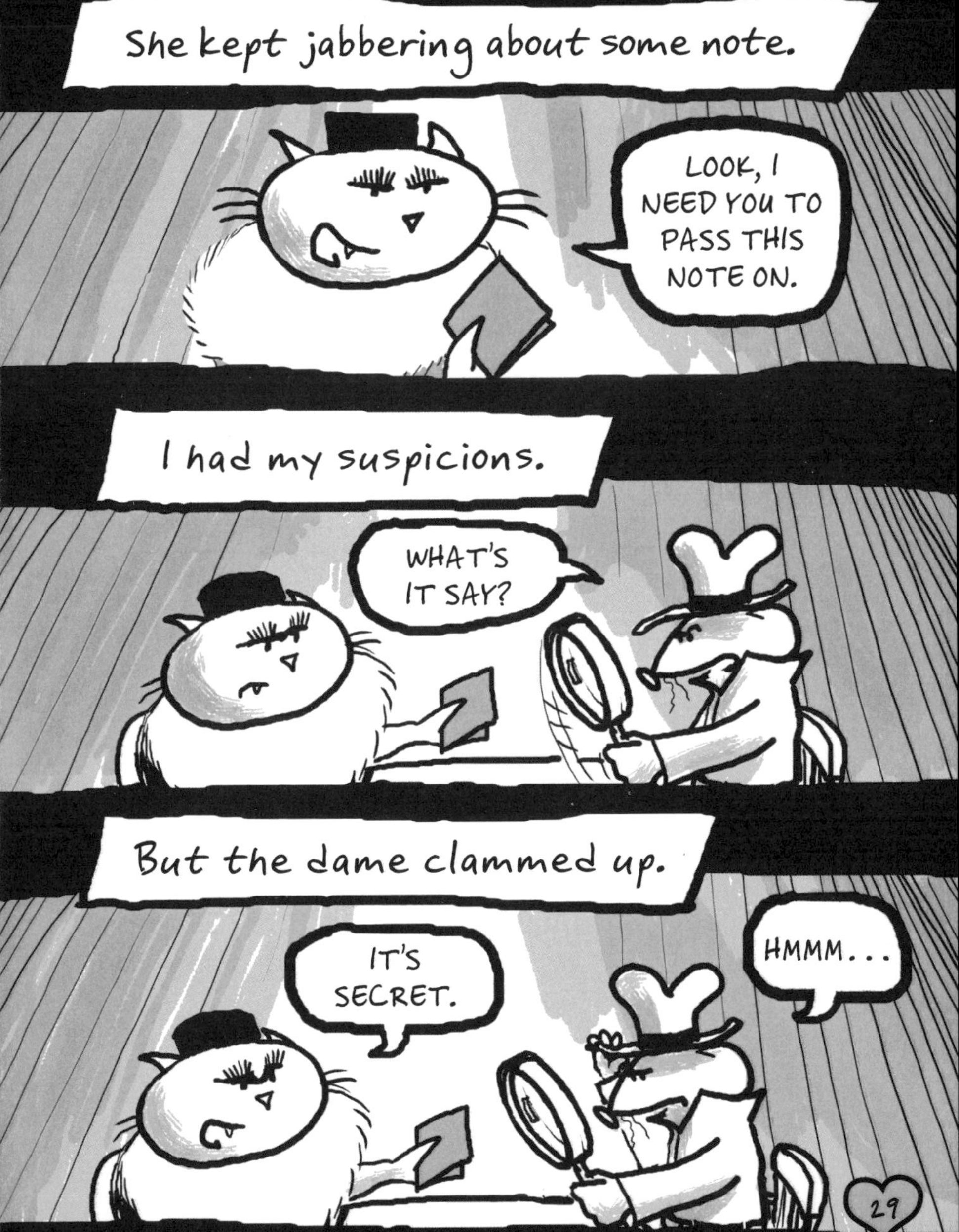
She kept jabbering about some note.
LOOK, I NEED YOU TO PASS THIS NOTE ON.
I had my suspicions.
WHAT'S IT SAY?
But the dame clammed up.
IT'S SECRET.
HMMM...

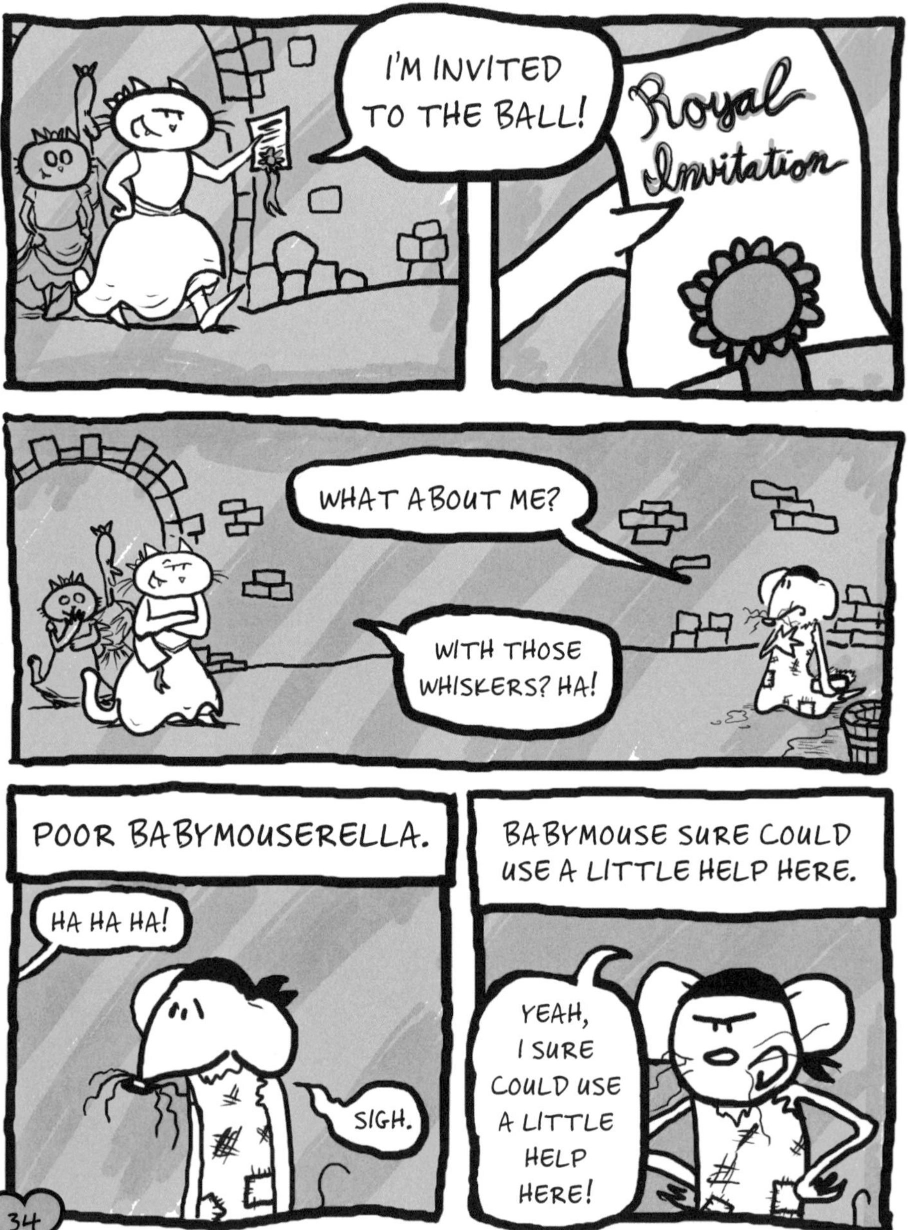
I'M INVITED TO THE BALL!
Royal Invitation
WHAT ABOUT ME?
WITH THOSE WHISKERS? HA!
POOR BABYMOUSERELLA.
HA HA HA!
SIGH.
BABYMOUSE SURE COULD USE A LITTLE HELP HERE.
YEAH, I SURE COULD USE A LITTLE HELP HERE!

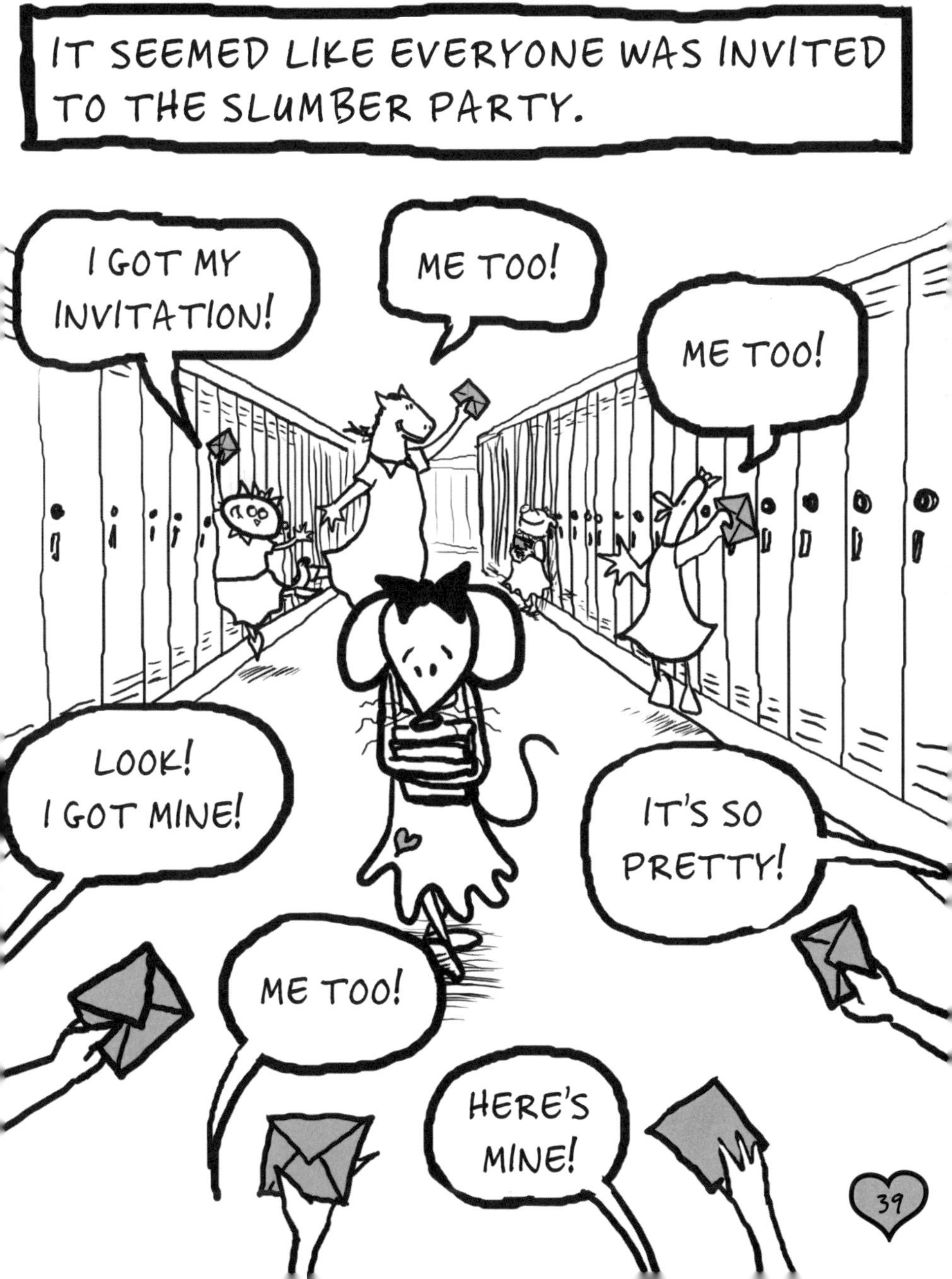
IT SEEMED LIKE EVERYONE WAS INVITED TO THE SLUMBER PARTY.
I GOT MY INVITATION!
ME TOO!
ME TOO!
LOOK! I GOT MINE!
IT'S SO PRETTY!
ME TOO!
HERE'S MINE!

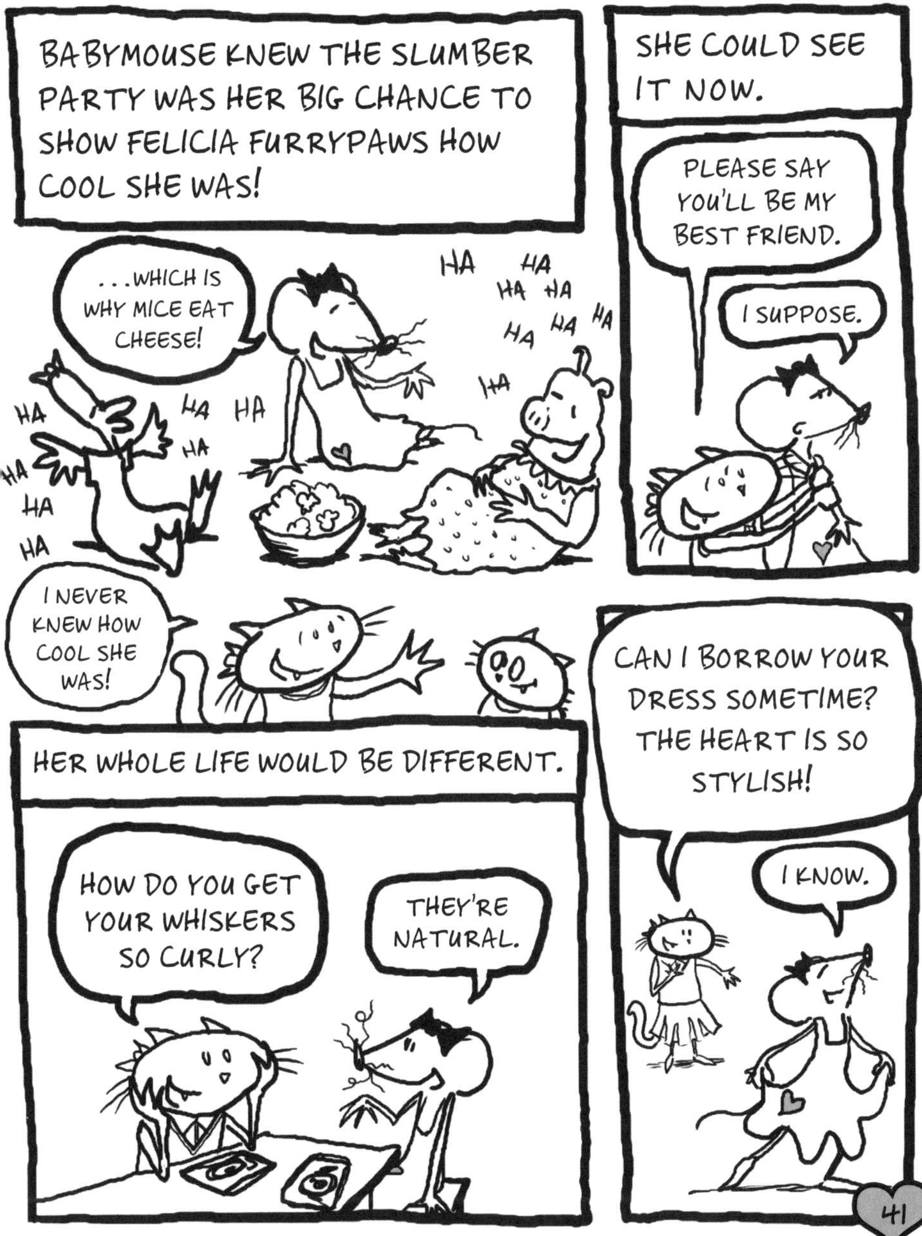
BABYMOUSE KNEW THE SLUMBER PARTY WAS HER BIG CHANCE TO SHOW FELICIA FURRYPAWS HOW COOL SHE WAS!
. . .WHICH IS WHY MICE EAT CHEESE!
HA HA HA HA HA HA HA HA HA
HA HA HA HA HA HA HA
SHE COULD SEE IT NOW.
PLEASE SAY YOU'LL BE MY BEST FRIEND.
I SUPPOSE.
I NEVER KNEW HOW COOL SHE WAS!
HER WHOLE LIFE WOULD BE DIFFERENT.
HOW DO YOU GET YOUR WHISKERS SO CURLY?
THEY'RE NATURAL.
CAN I BORROW YOUR DRESS SOMETIME? THE HEART IS SO STYLISH!
I KNOW.

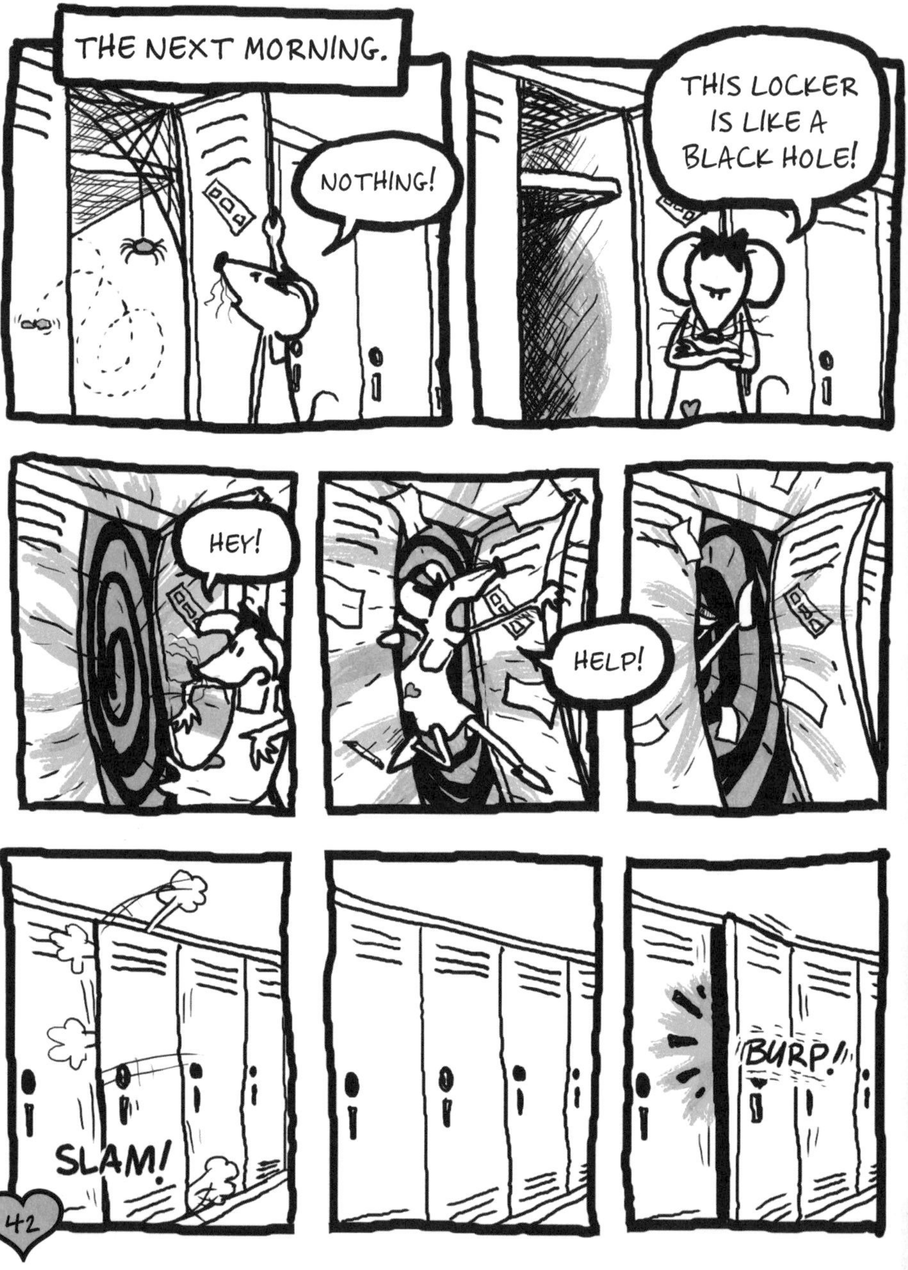
THE NEXT MORNING.
NOTHING!
THIS LOCKER IS LIKE A BLACK HOLE!
HEY!
HELP!
SLAM!
BURP!

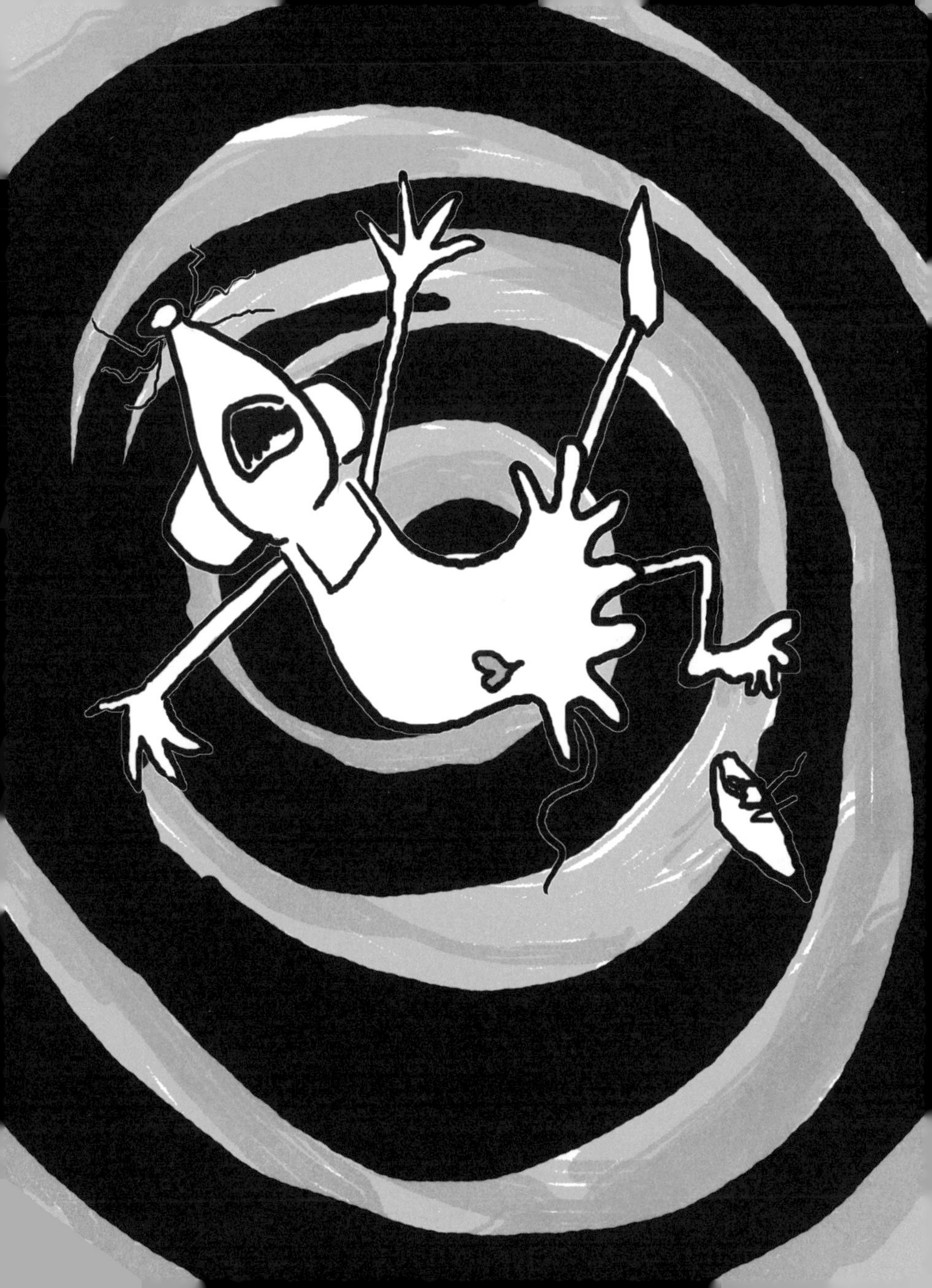

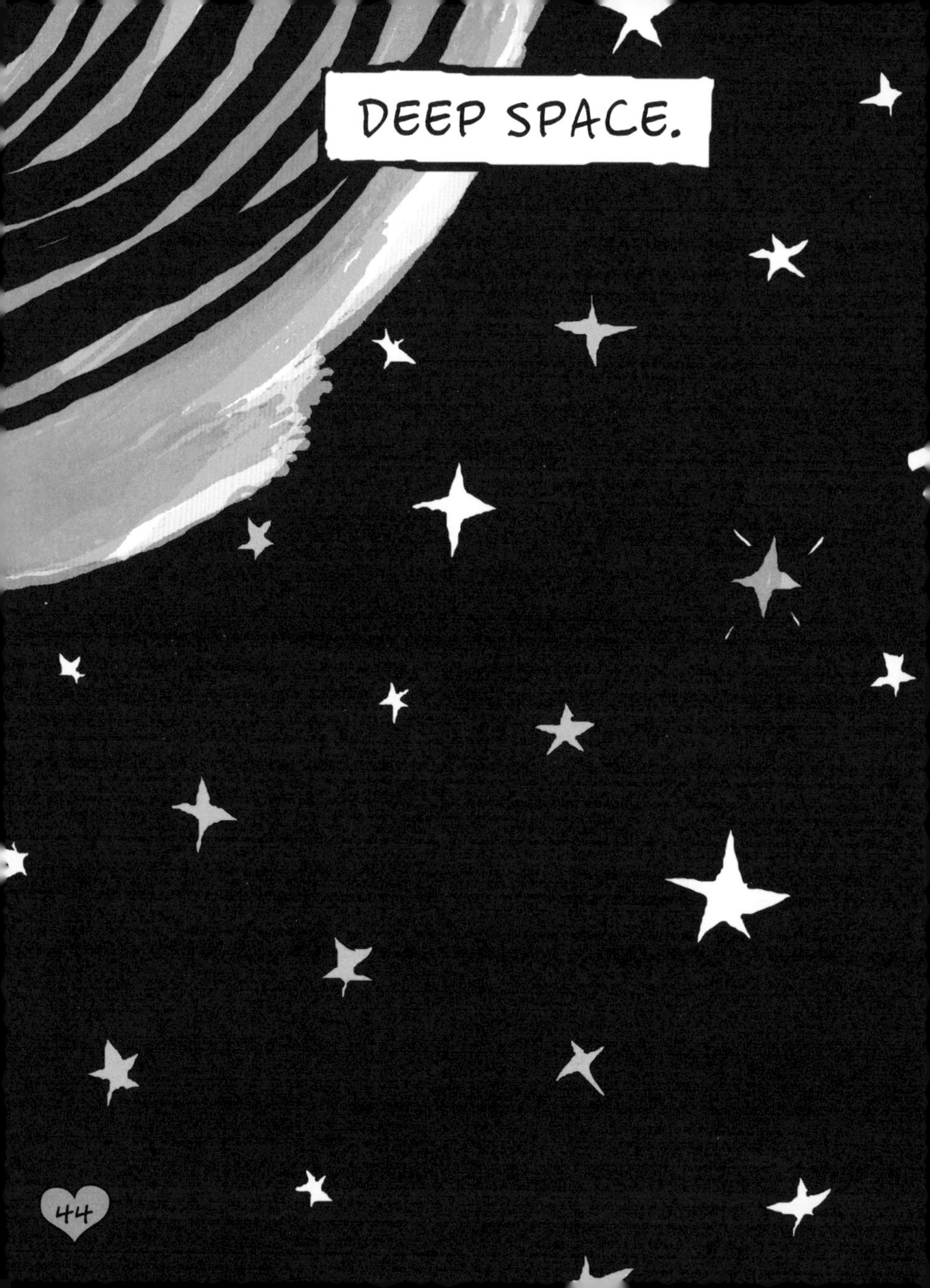
DEEP SPACE.

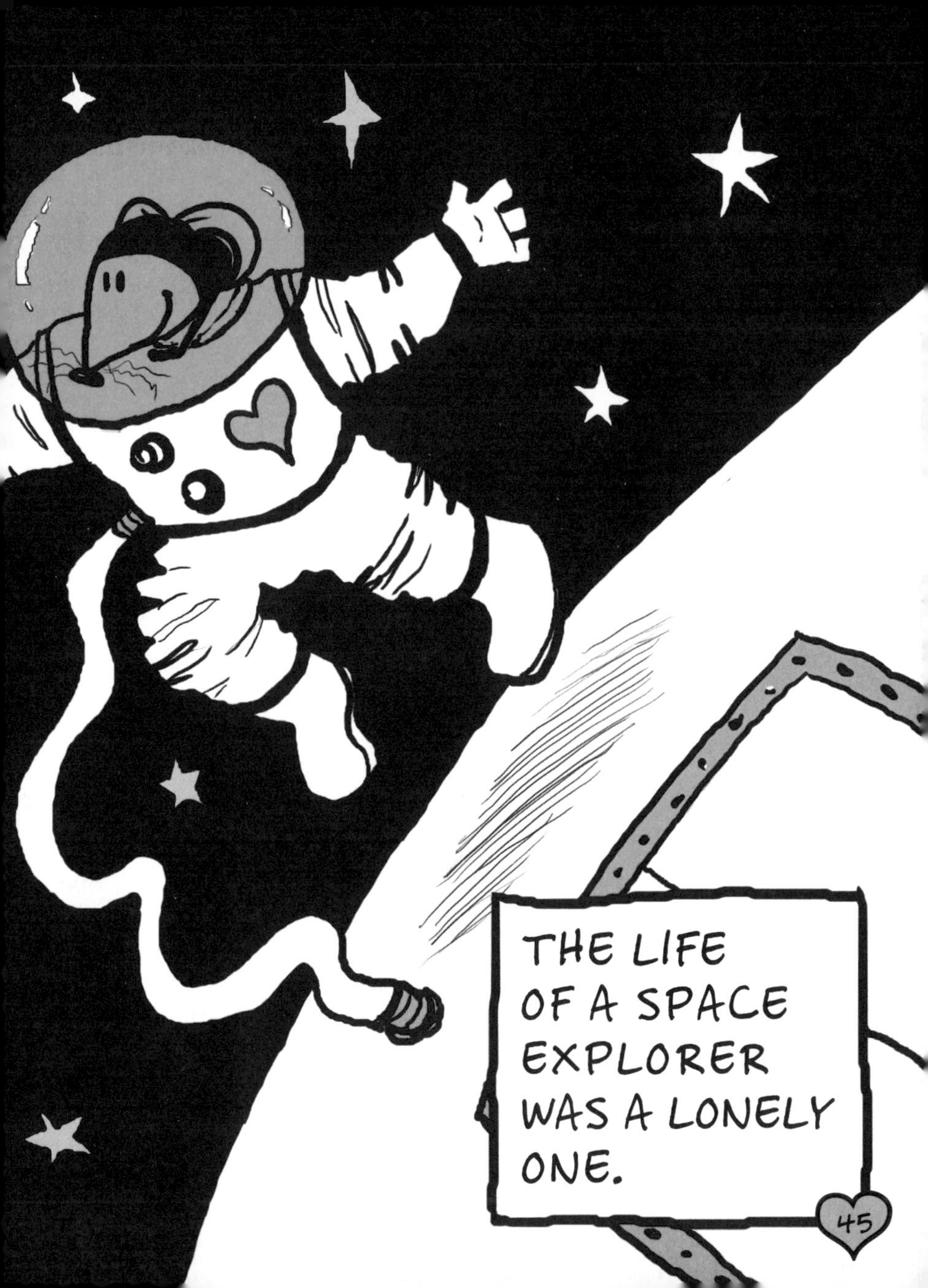
THE LIFE OF A SPACE EXPLORER WAS A LONELY ONE.

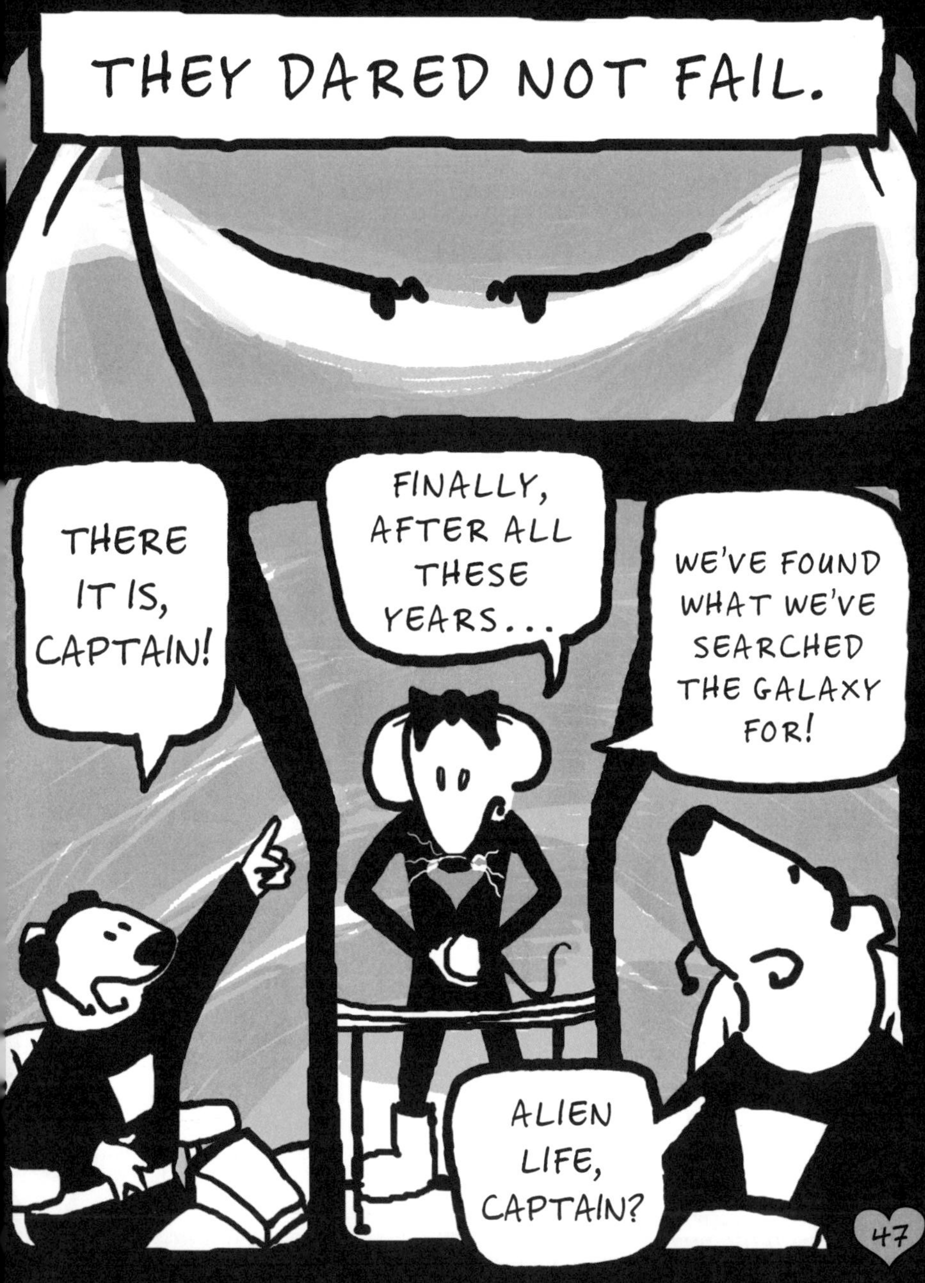
THEY DARED NOT FAIL.
THERE IT IS, CAPTAIN!
FINALLY, AFTER ALL THESE YEARS...
WE'VE FOUND WHAT WE'VE SEARCHED THE GALAXY FOR!
ALIEN LIFE, CAPTAIN?

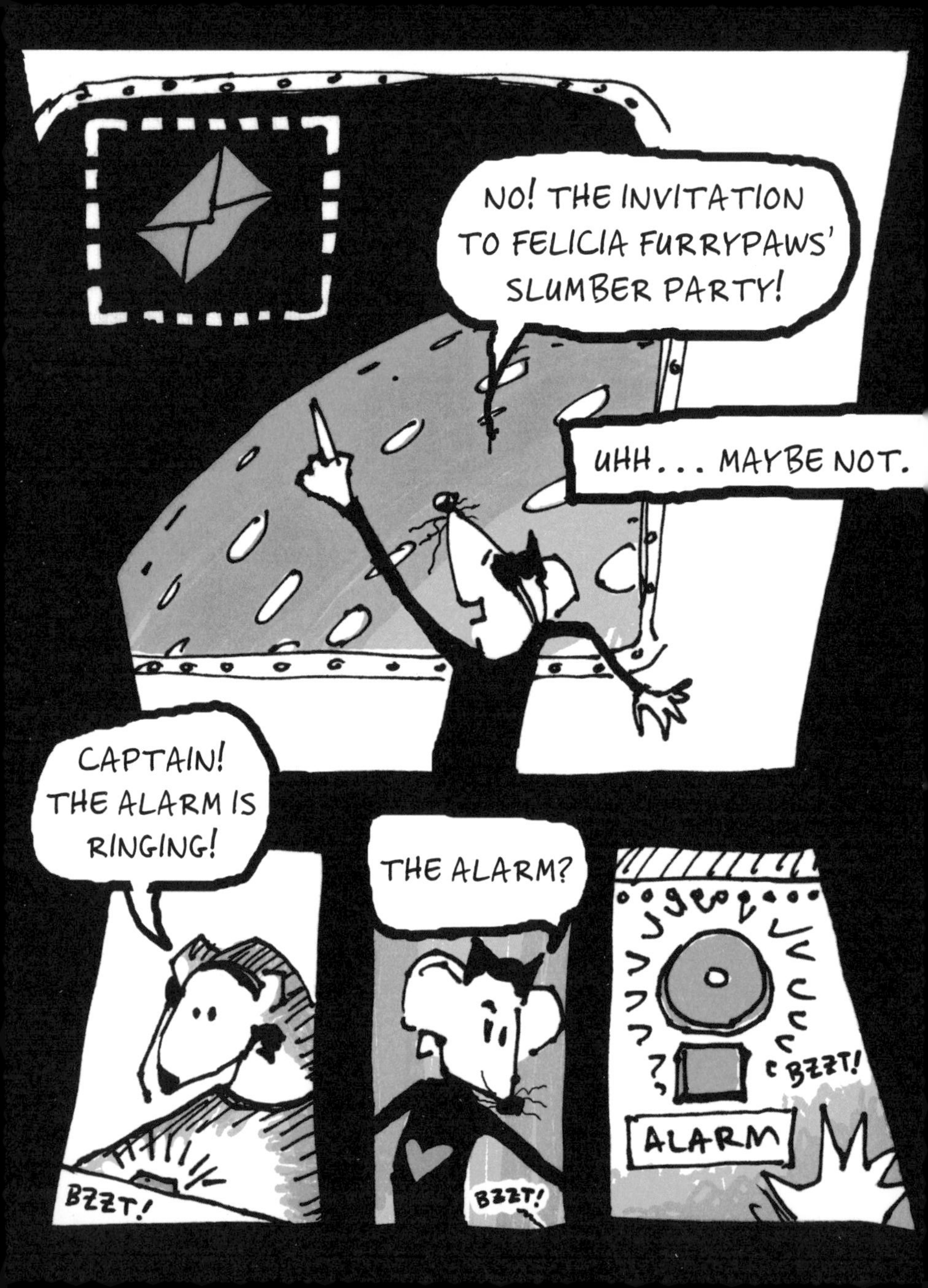
NO! THE INVITATION TO FELICIA FURRYPAWS' SLUMBER PARTY!
UHH . . . MAYBE NOT.
CAPTAIN! THE ALARM IS RINGING!
BZZT!
THE ALARM?
BZZT!
BZZT!
ALARM

BABYMOUSE MADE PLANS.

STEP #1.

I DON'T EAT CUPCAKES.

BUT THEY'RE REALLY YUMMY!

STEP #2.

I DON'T LIKE TO READ.

BUT IT'S REALLY EXCITING!

NEW BOOK

BABYMOUSE DIDN'T GIVE UP EASILY.

THERE HAS TO BE **SOMETHING**.

OPERATION: SLEEPOVER
1. CUPCAKE
2. BOOK
FUNNY JOKE
COMPLIMENT

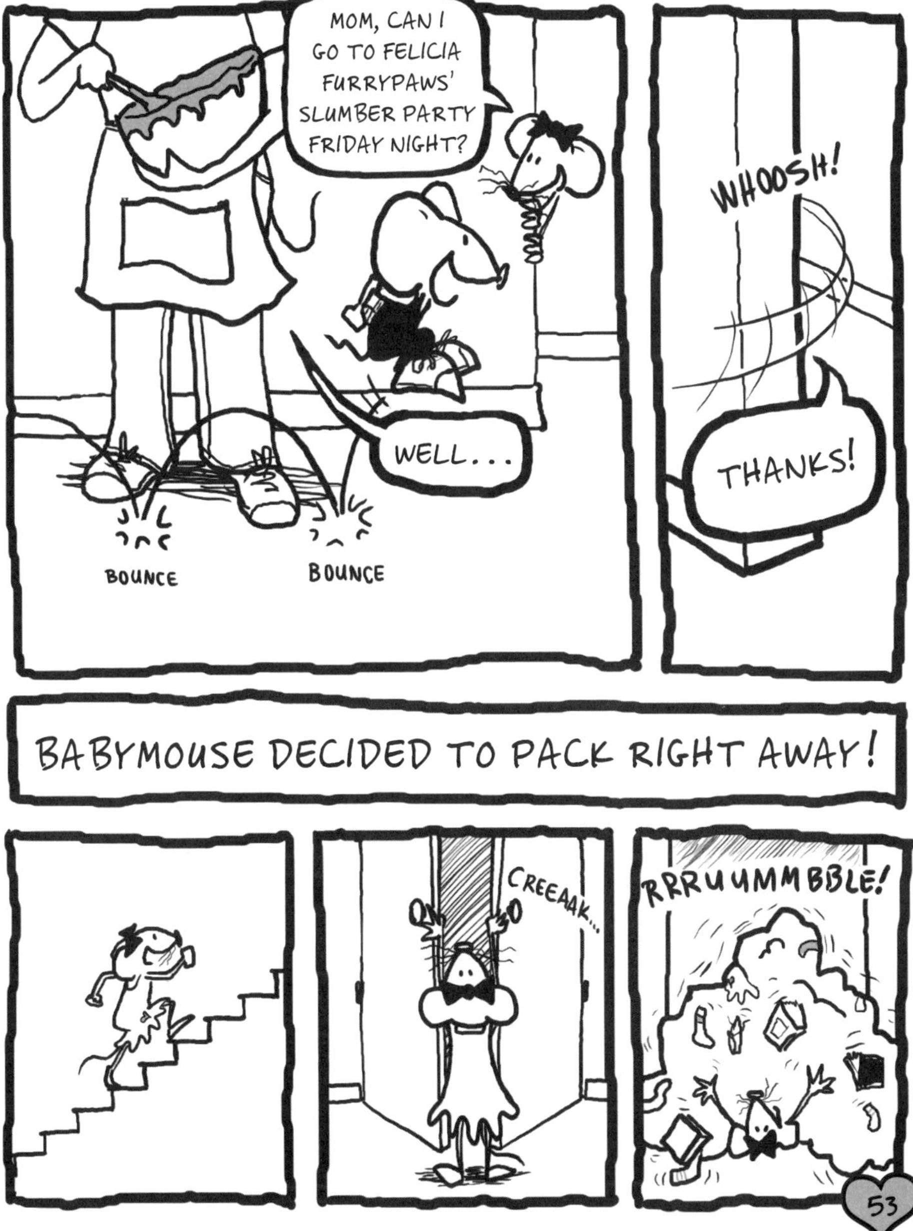
MOM, CAN I GO TO FELICIA FURRYPAWS' SLUMBER PARTY FRIDAY NIGHT?
WELL...
BOUNCE
BOUNCE
WHOOSH!
THANKS!
BABYMOUSE DECIDED TO PACK RIGHT AWAY!
CREEAAK...
RRRUUMMBBLE!

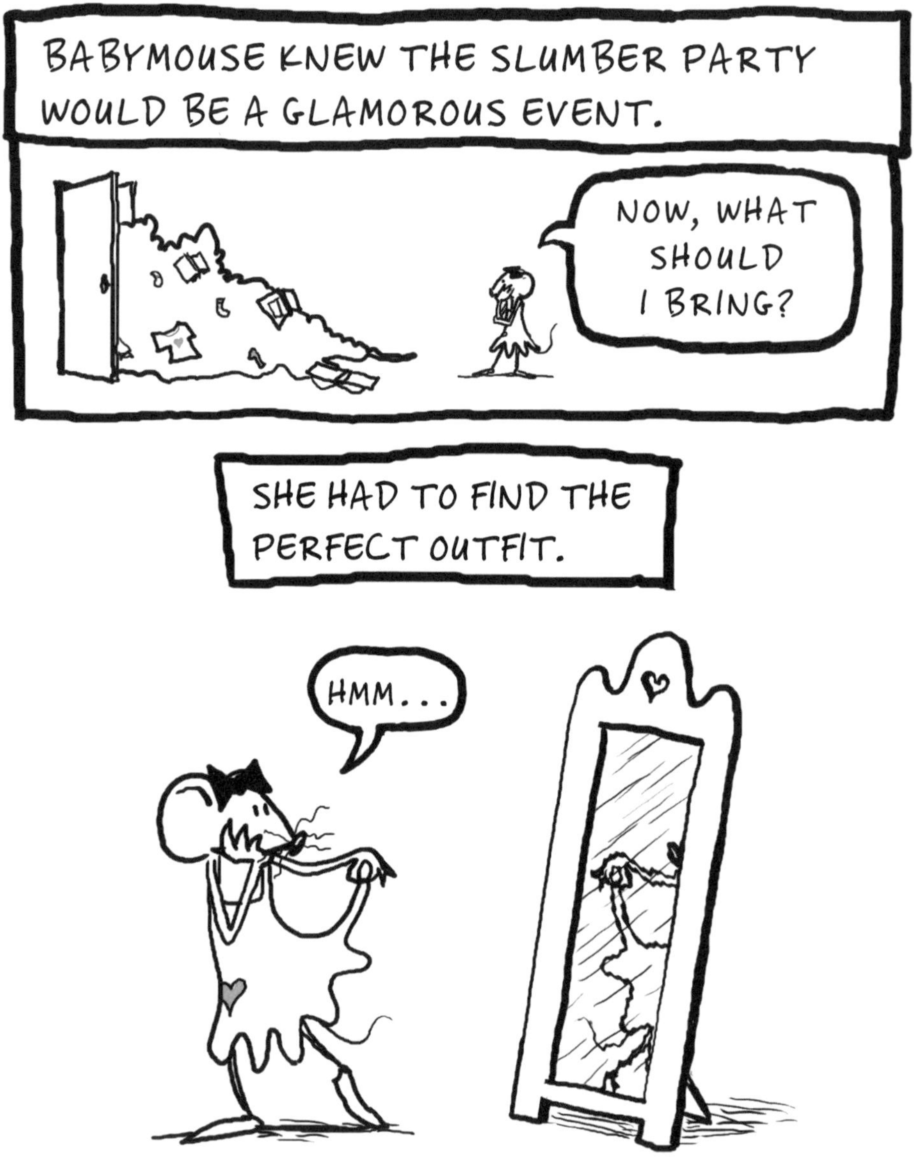
BABYMOUSE KNEW THE SLUMBER PARTY WOULD BE A GLAMOROUS EVENT.
NOW, WHAT SHOULD I BRING?
SHE HAD TO FIND THE PERFECT OUTFIT.
HMM...

TOO TIGHT.

GULP! ... CAN'T... BREATHE...

TOO FLUFFY.

BLEAH!

TOO DANGEROUS!

WHA-

UH-OH

WHOA!

AAAAAAH!

WHUMP!

TOO CONFUSING!

I'M DIZZY!

PERFECT!

55

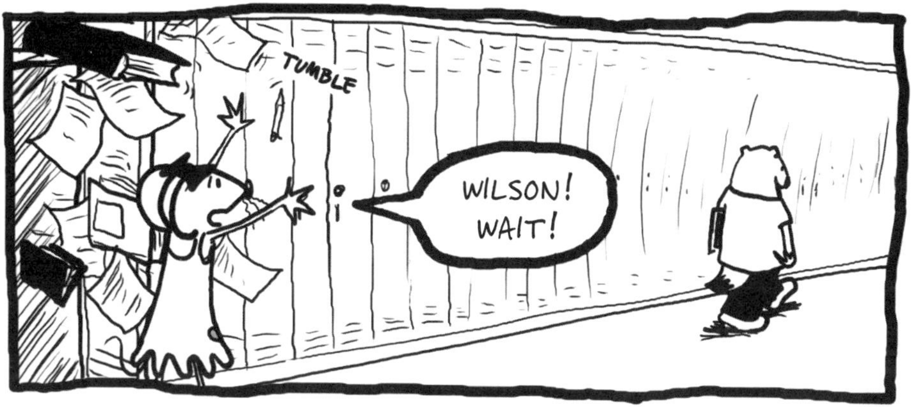
TUMBLE
WILSON! WAIT!

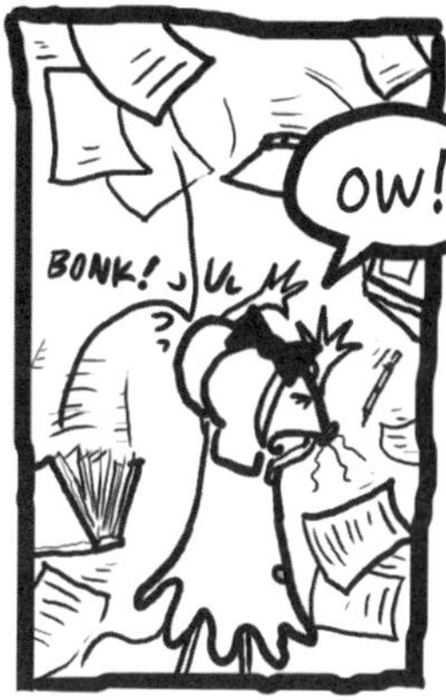
OW!
BONK!

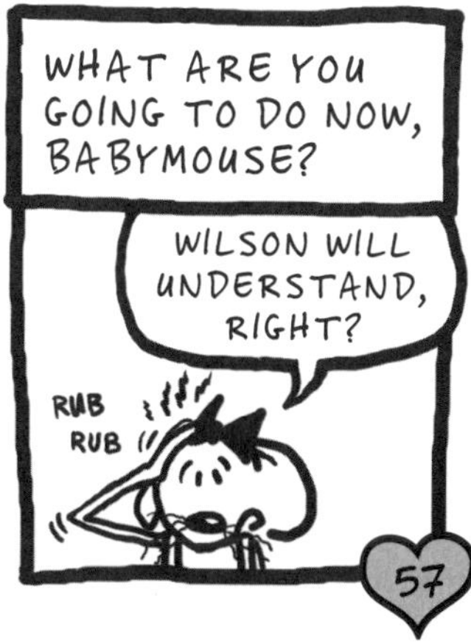
WHAT ARE YOU GOING TO DO NOW, BABYMOUSE?
WILSON WILL UNDERSTAND, RIGHT?
RUB RUB

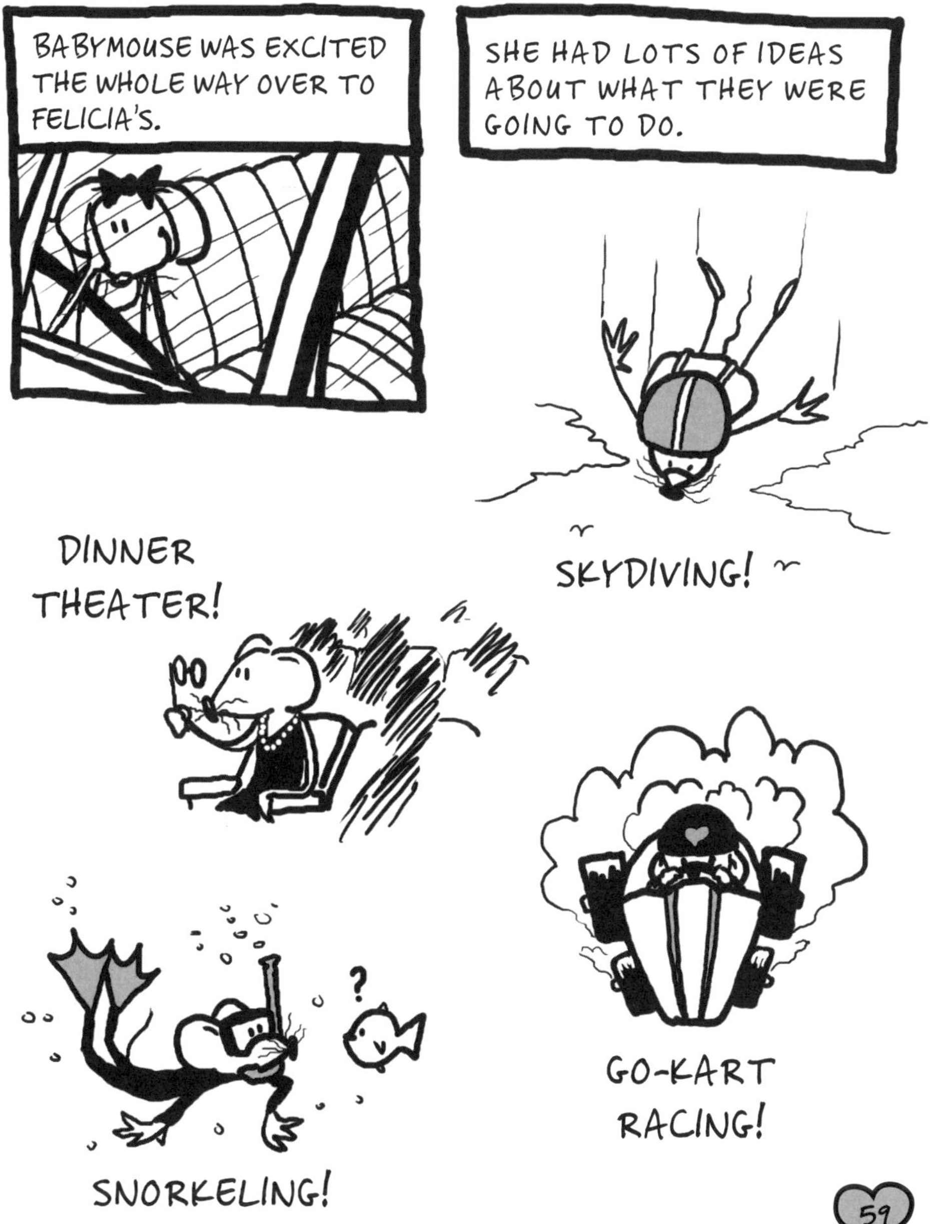
BABYMOUSE WAS EXCITED THE WHOLE WAY OVER TO FELICIA'S.
SHE HAD LOTS OF IDEAS ABOUT WHAT THEY WERE GOING TO DO.
SKYDIVING!
DINNER THEATER!
GO-KART RACING!
?
SNORKELING!

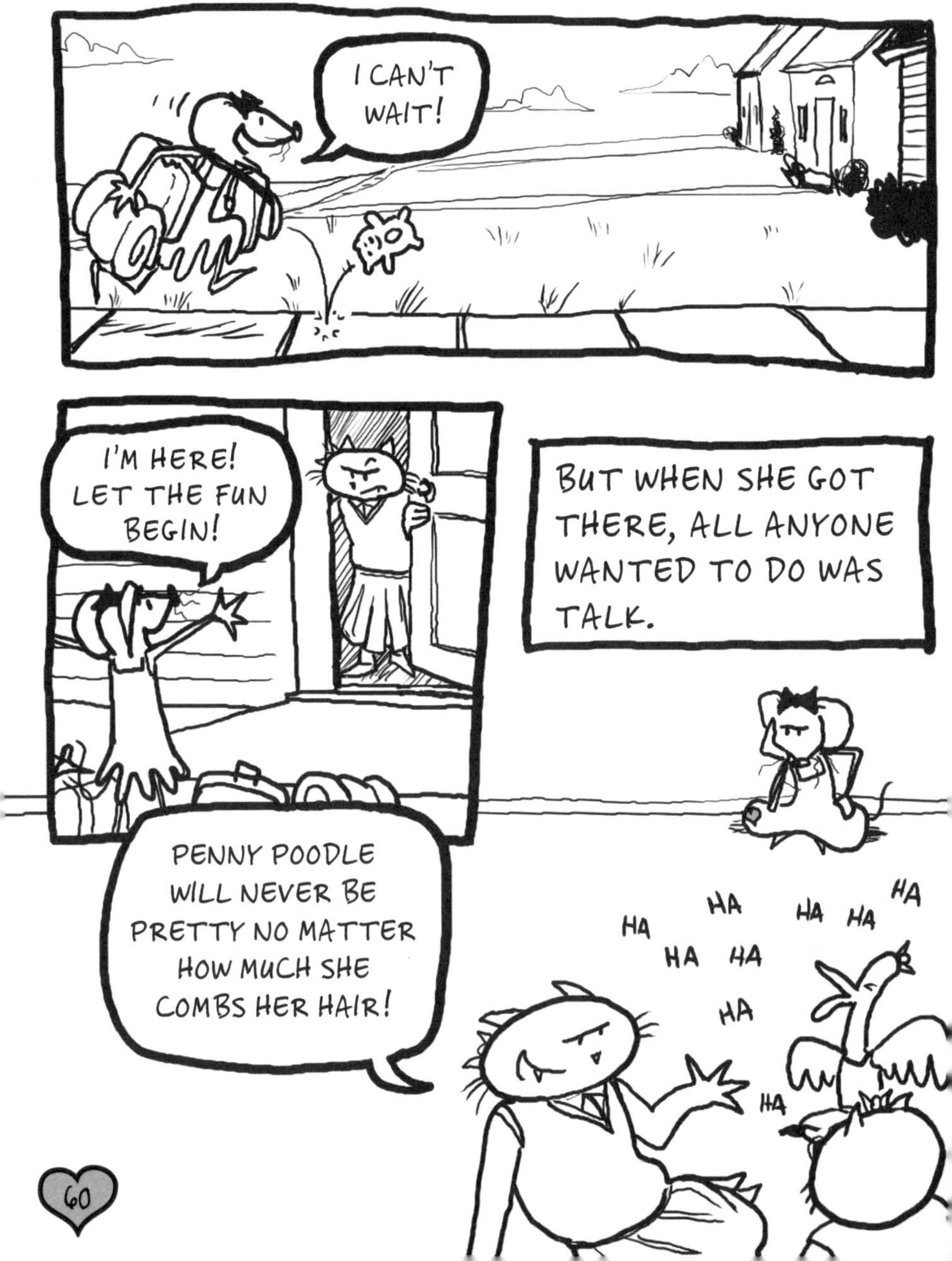
I CAN'T WAIT!
I'M HERE! LET THE FUN BEGIN!
BUT WHEN SHE GOT THERE, ALL ANYONE WANTED TO DO WAS TALK.
PENNY POODLE WILL NEVER BE PRETTY NO MATTER HOW MUCH SHE COMBS HER HAIR!
HA HA HA HA HA HA HA HA HA HA

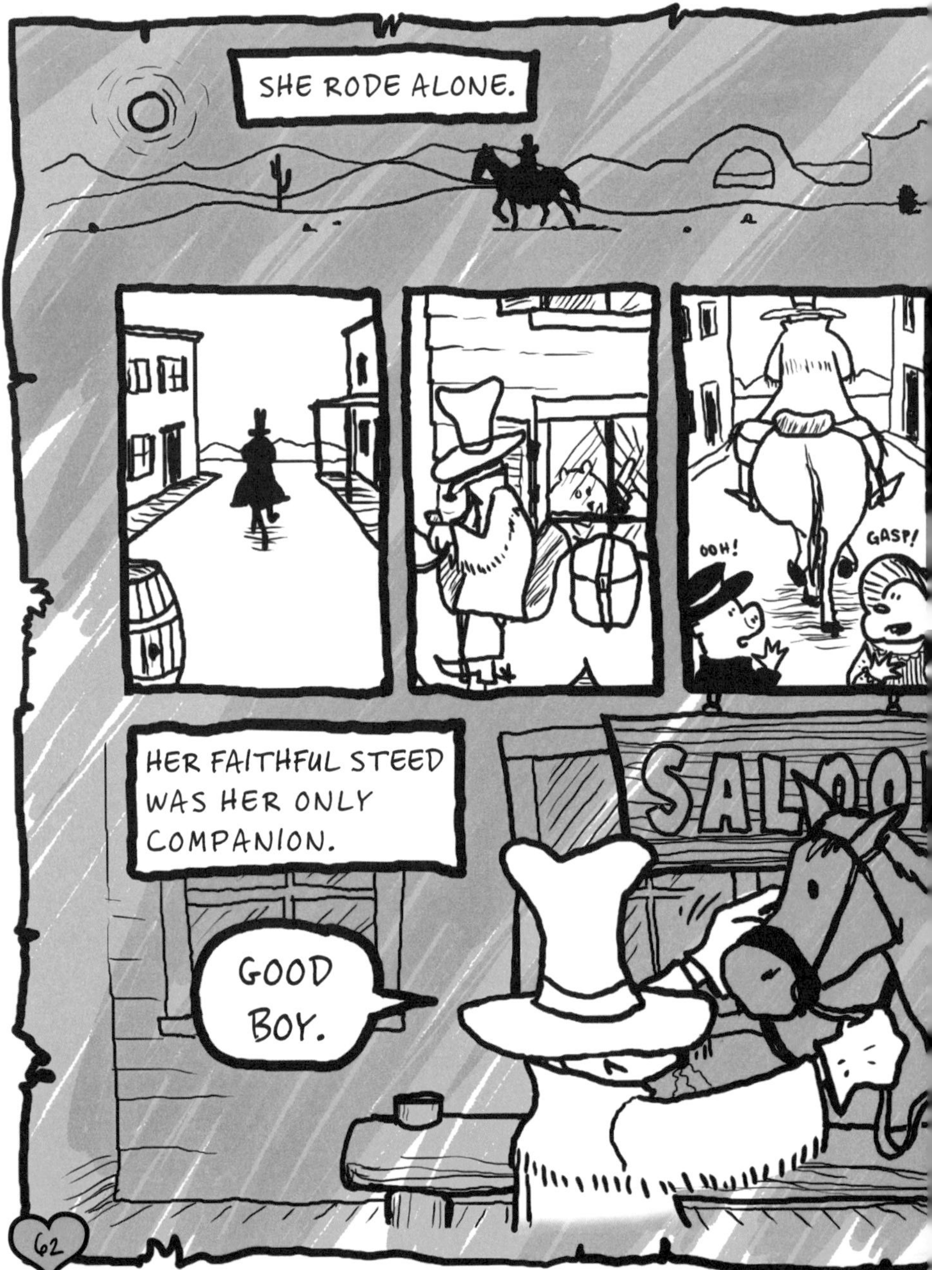
SHE RODE ALONE.
OOH!
GASP!
SAL
HER FAITHFUL STEED WAS HER ONLY COMPANION.
GOOD BOY.

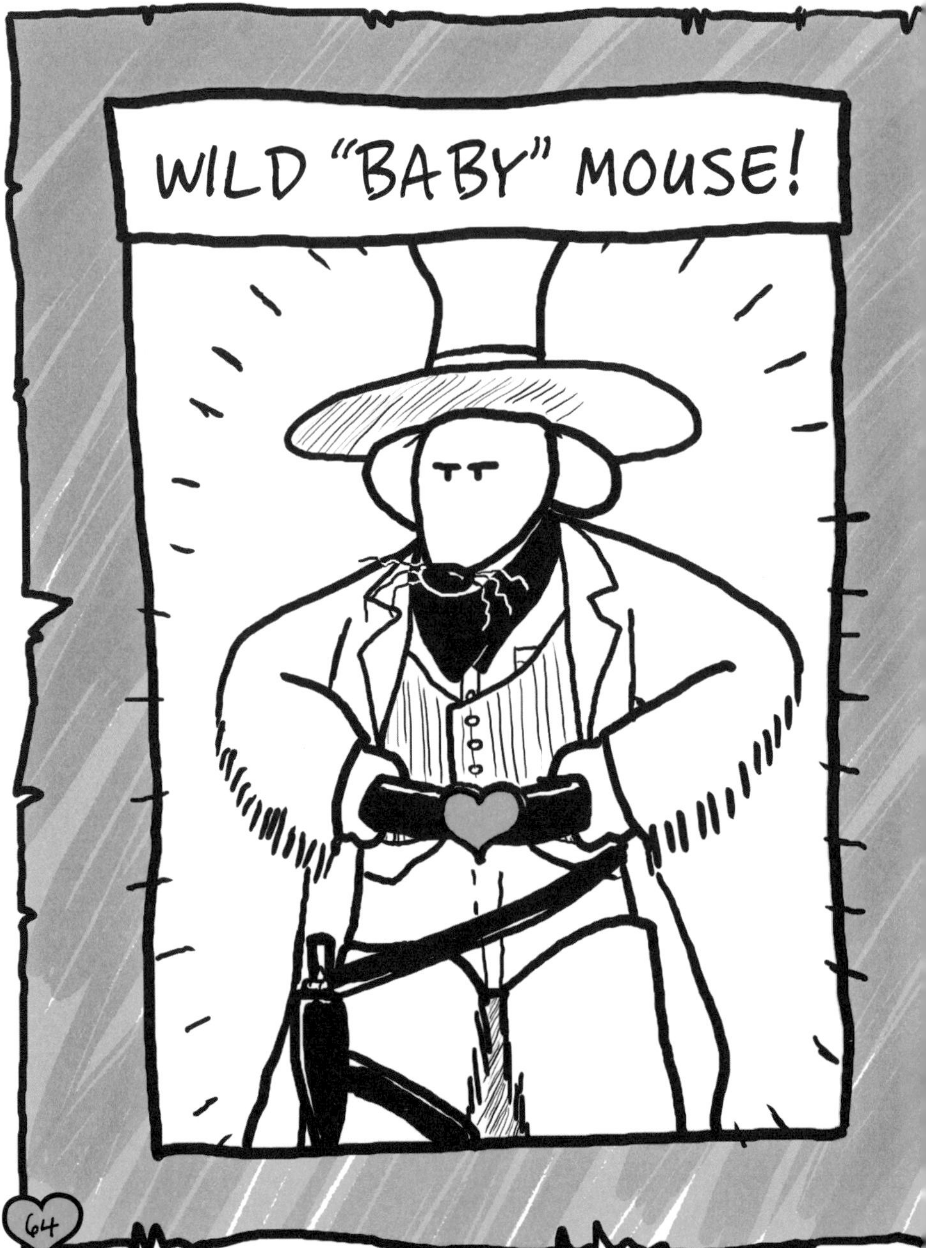
WILD "BABY" MOUSE!

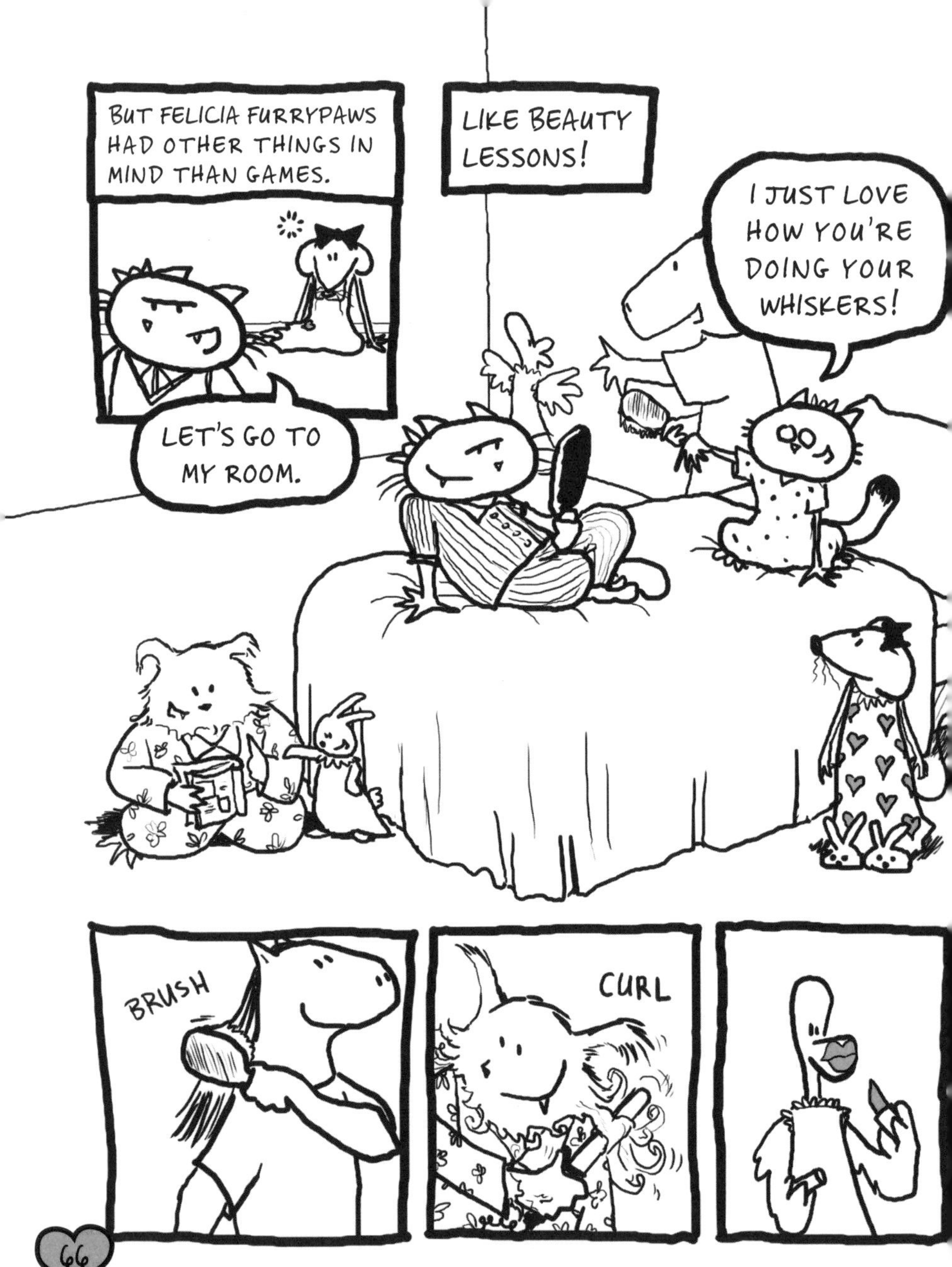

BUT FELICIA FURRYPAWS HAD OTHER THINGS IN MIND THAN GAMES.
LET'S GO TO MY ROOM.
LIKE BEAUTY LESSONS!
I JUST LOVE HOW YOU'RE DOING YOUR WHISKERS!
BRUSH
CURL

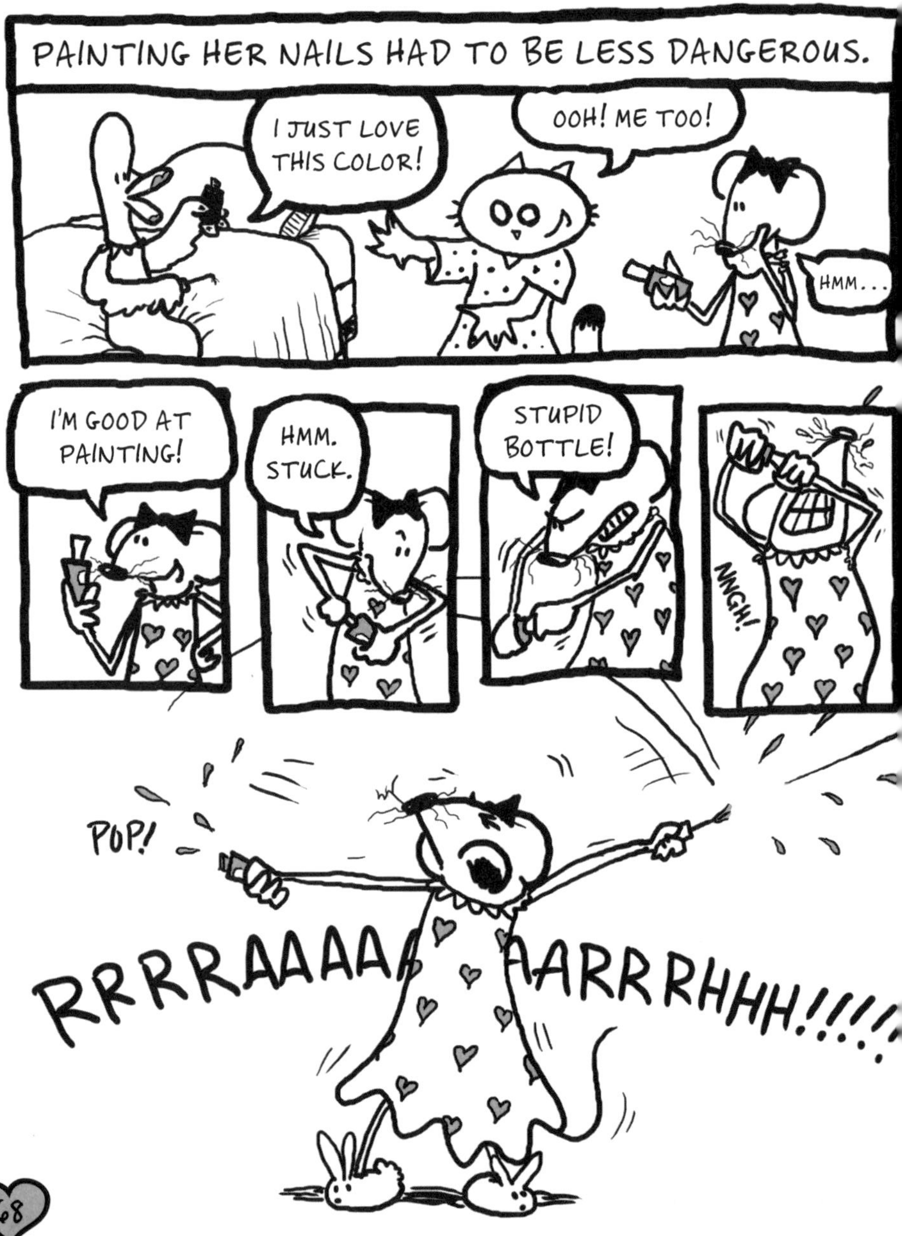
PAINTING HER NAILS HAD TO BE LESS DANGEROUS.
I JUST LOVE THIS COLOR!
OOH! ME TOO!
HMM...
I'M GOOD AT PAINTING!
HMM. STUCK.
STUPID BOTTLE!
NNGH!
POP!
RRRRAAAAAAARRRRHHH!!!!!!

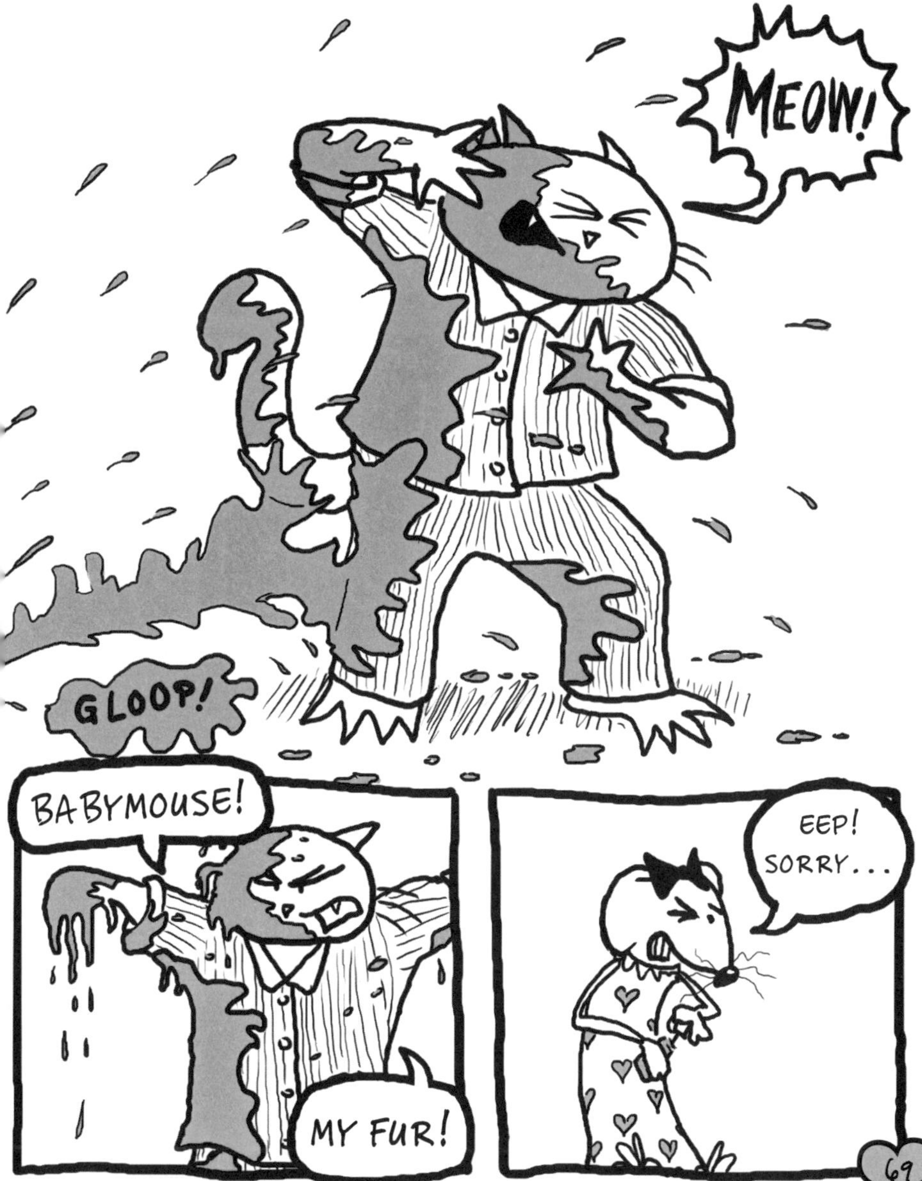
MEOW!
GLOOP!
BABYMOUSE!
MY FUR!
EEP! SORRY...

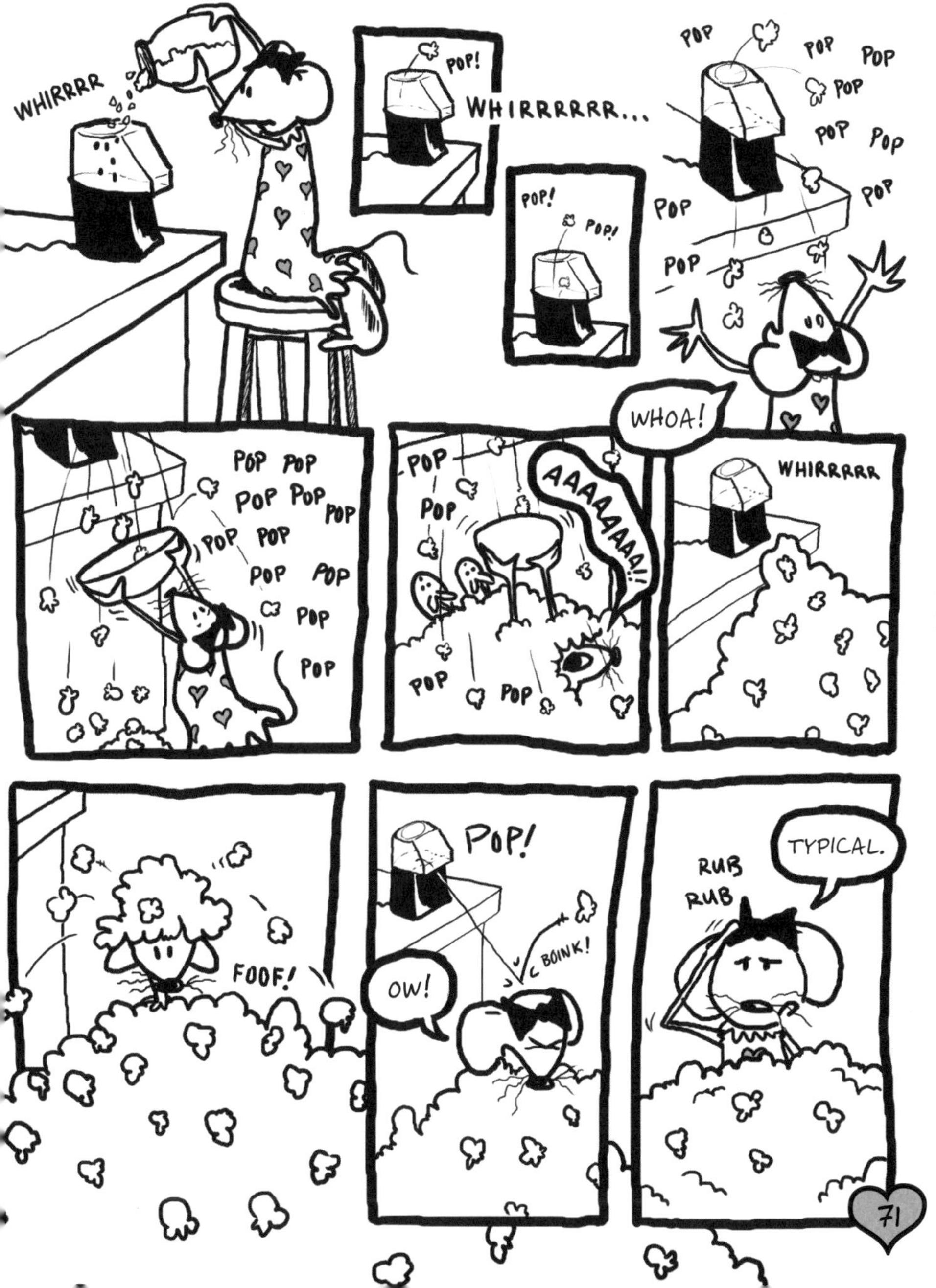
WHIRRRR
POP!
WHIRRRRRR...
POP!
POP!
POP POP POP POP POP POP POP POP POP
POP POP POP POP POP POP POP POP POP POP POP
WHOA!
POP
POP
AAAAAAAAA!!
POP POP
WHIRRRRR
FOOF!
POP!
BOINK!
OW!
RUB RUB
TYPICAL.

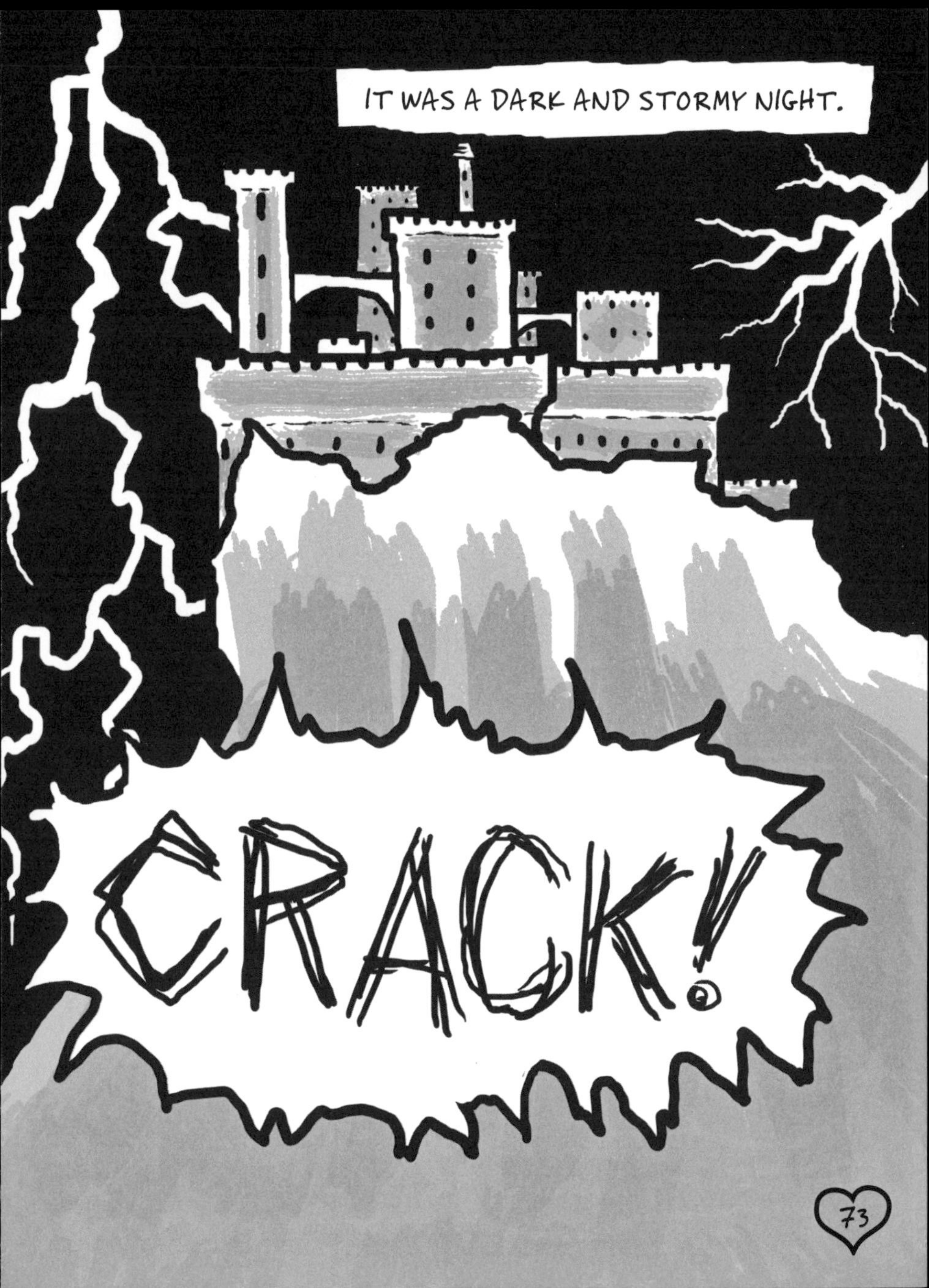
IT WAS A DARK AND STORMY NIGHT.
CRACK!

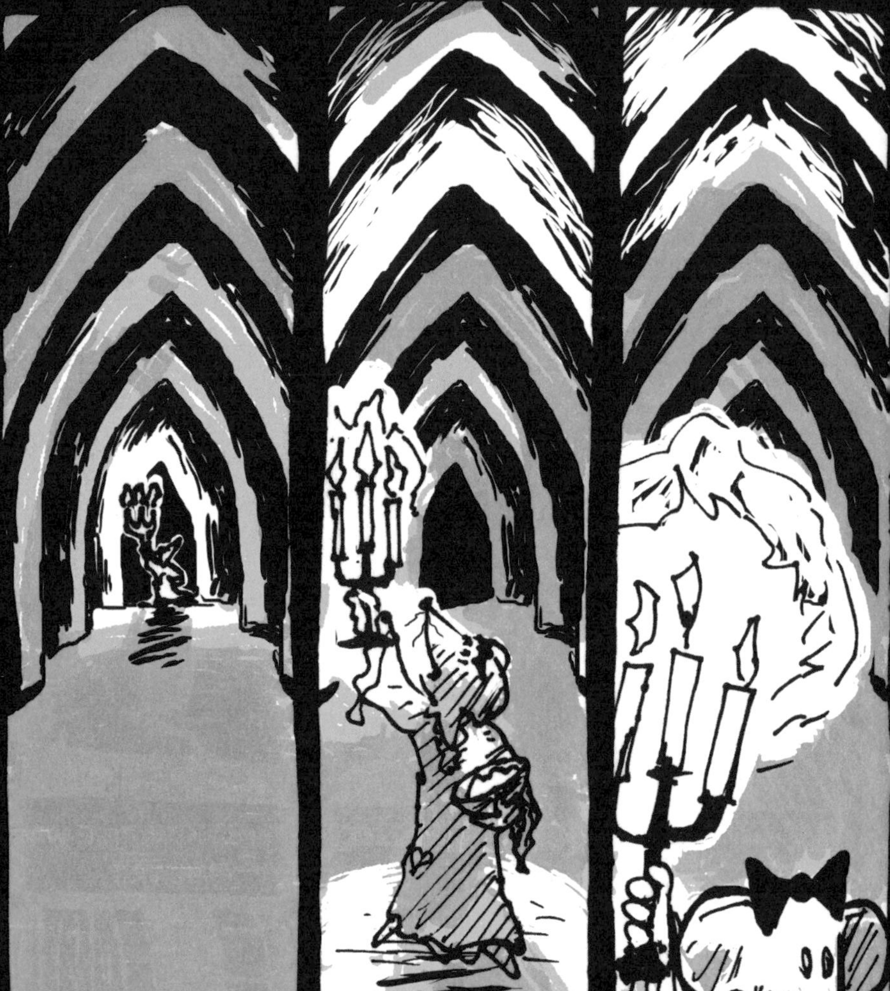
LADY BABYMOUSE HAD COME TO CASTLE WEASELSTEIN.

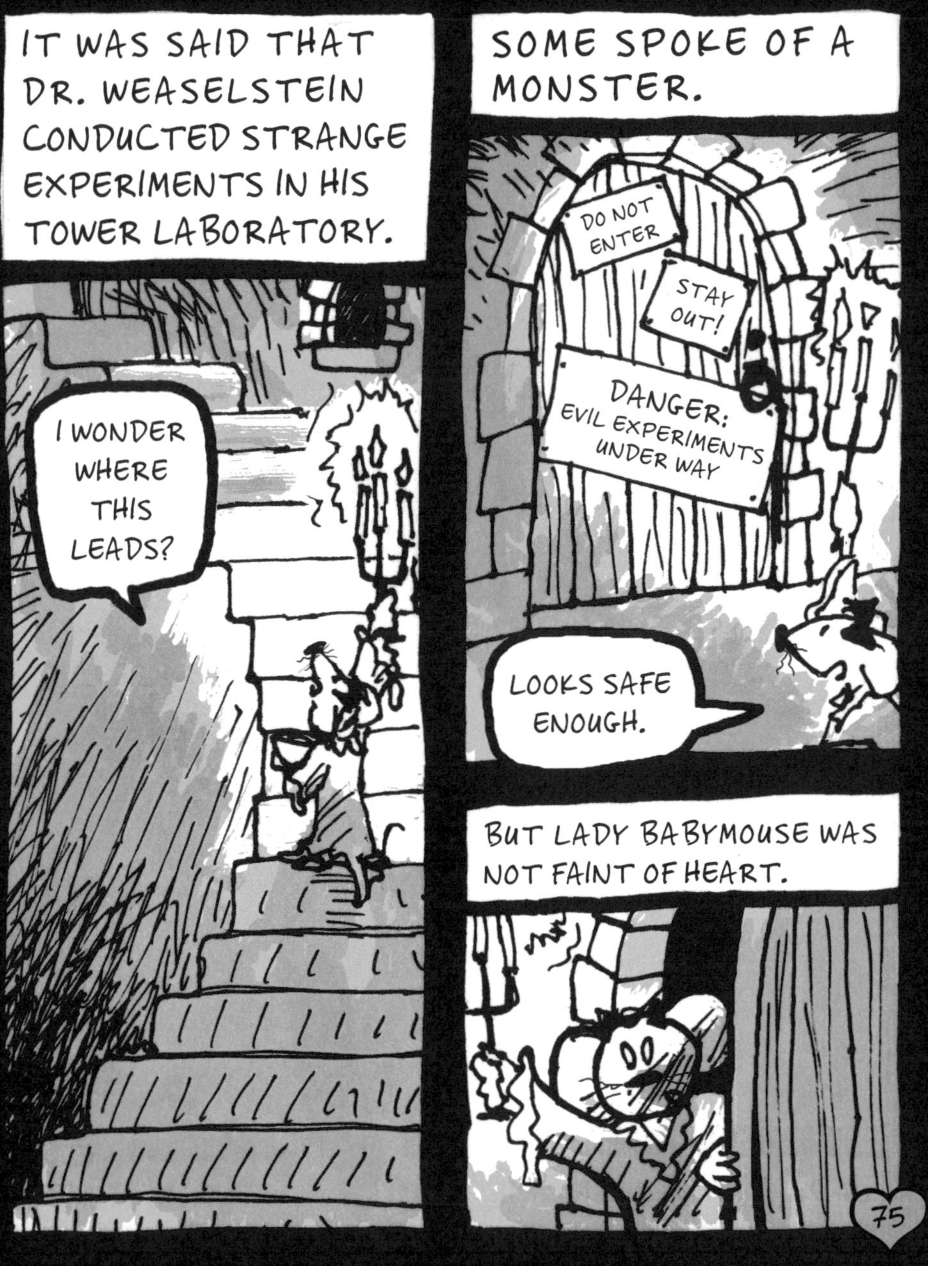
IT WAS SAID THAT DR. WEASELSTEIN CONDUCTED STRANGE EXPERIMENTS IN HIS TOWER LABORATORY.
I WONDER WHERE THIS LEADS?
SOME SPOKE OF A MONSTER.
DO NOT ENTER
STAY OUT!
DANGER: EVIL EXPERIMENTS UNDER WAY
LOOKS SAFE ENOUGH.
BUT LADY BABYMOUSE WAS NOT FAINT OF HEART.

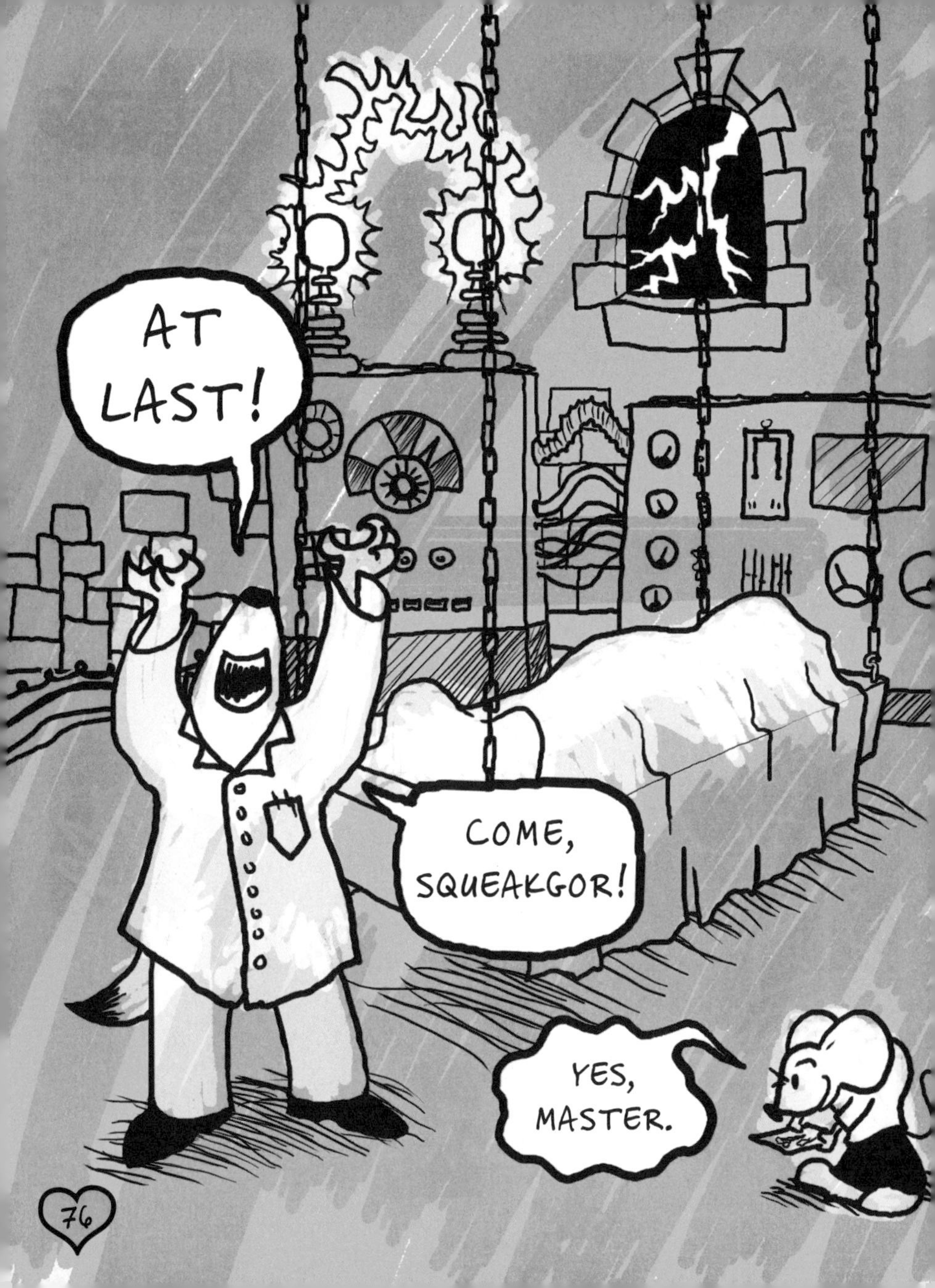
AT LAST!
COME, SQUEAKGOR!
YES, MASTER.

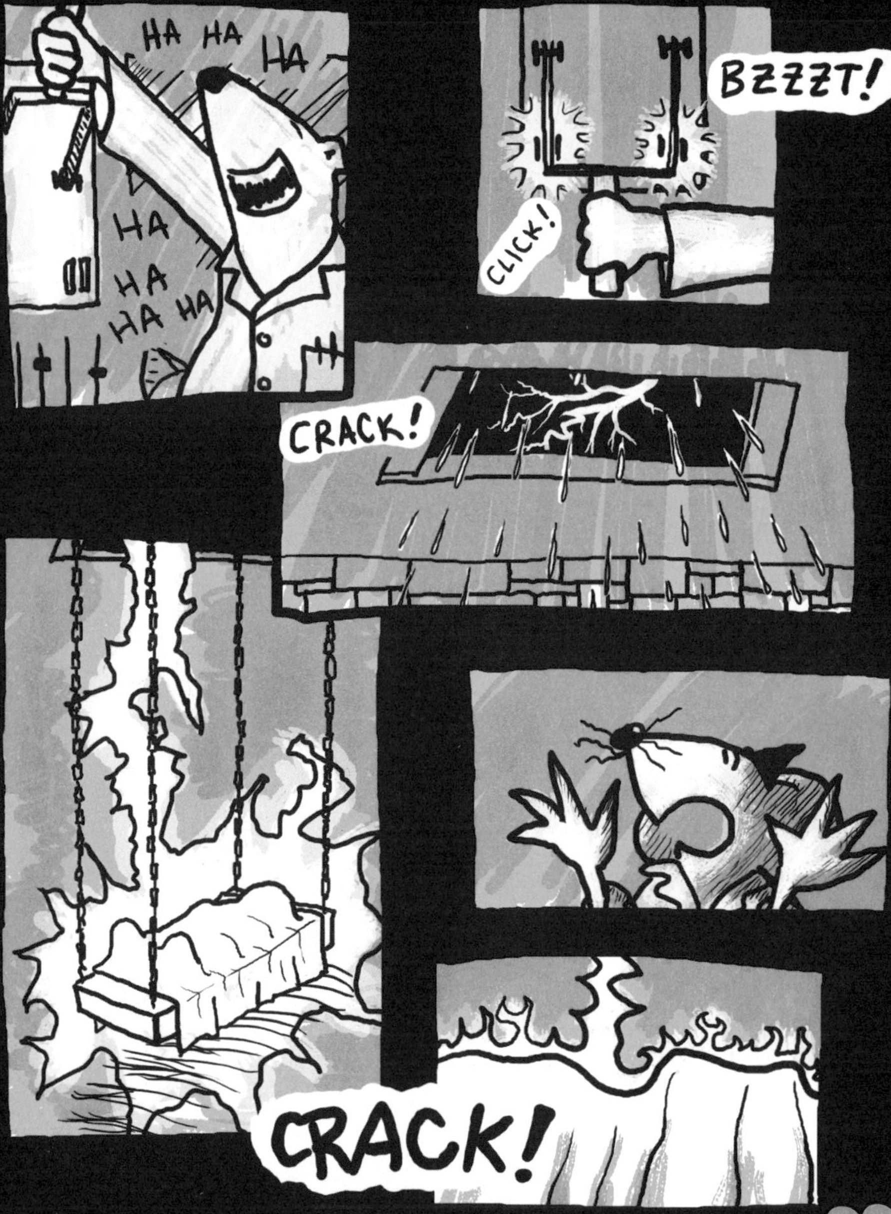
HA HA HA
HA
HA
HA HA
BZZZT!
CLICK!
CRACK!
CRACK!

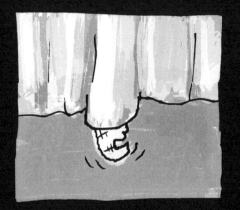

SHE'S ALIVE!

ALIVE!

GASP!

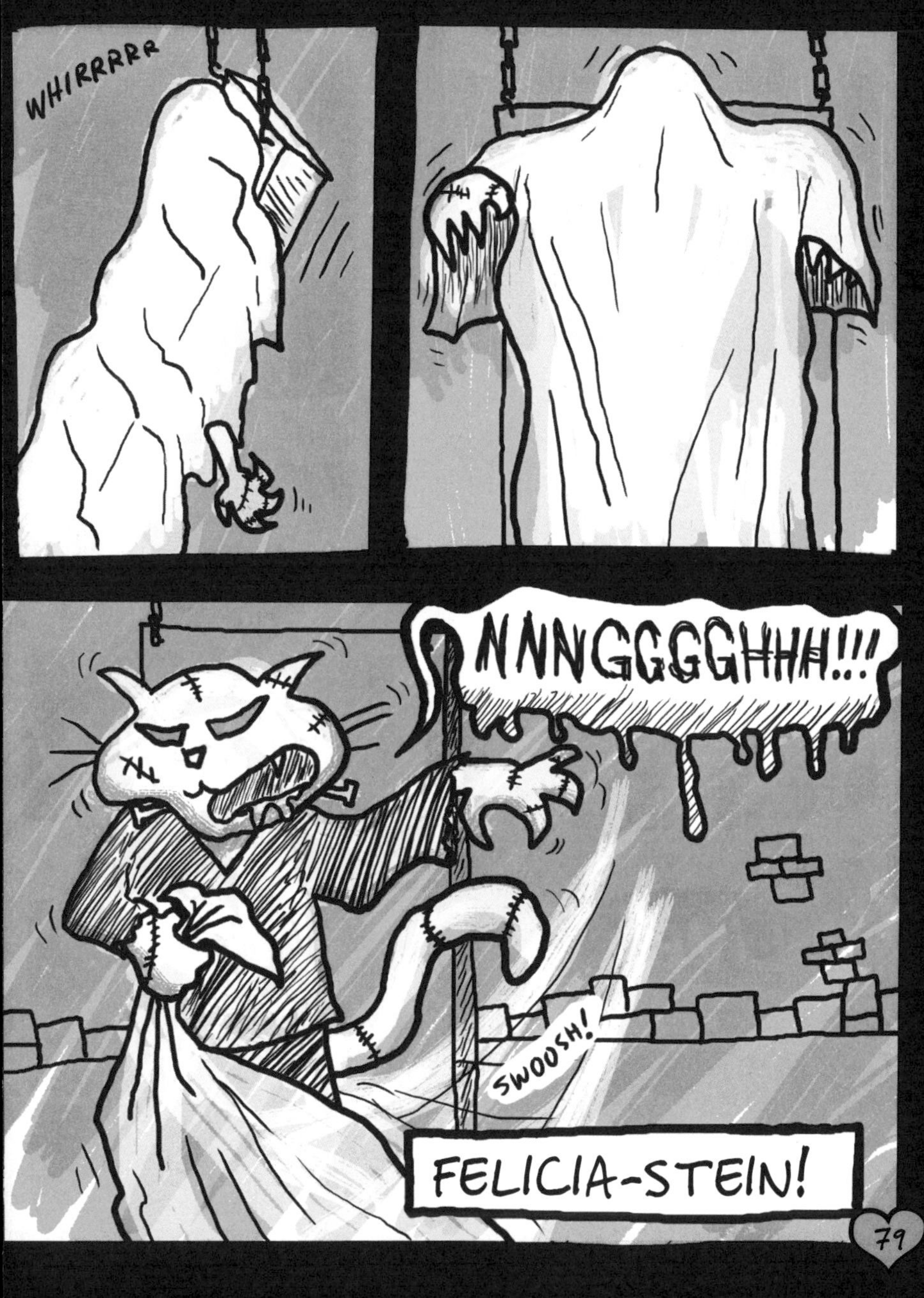
WHIRRRRR
NNNGGGGHHH!!!
SWOOSH!
FELICIA-STEIN!

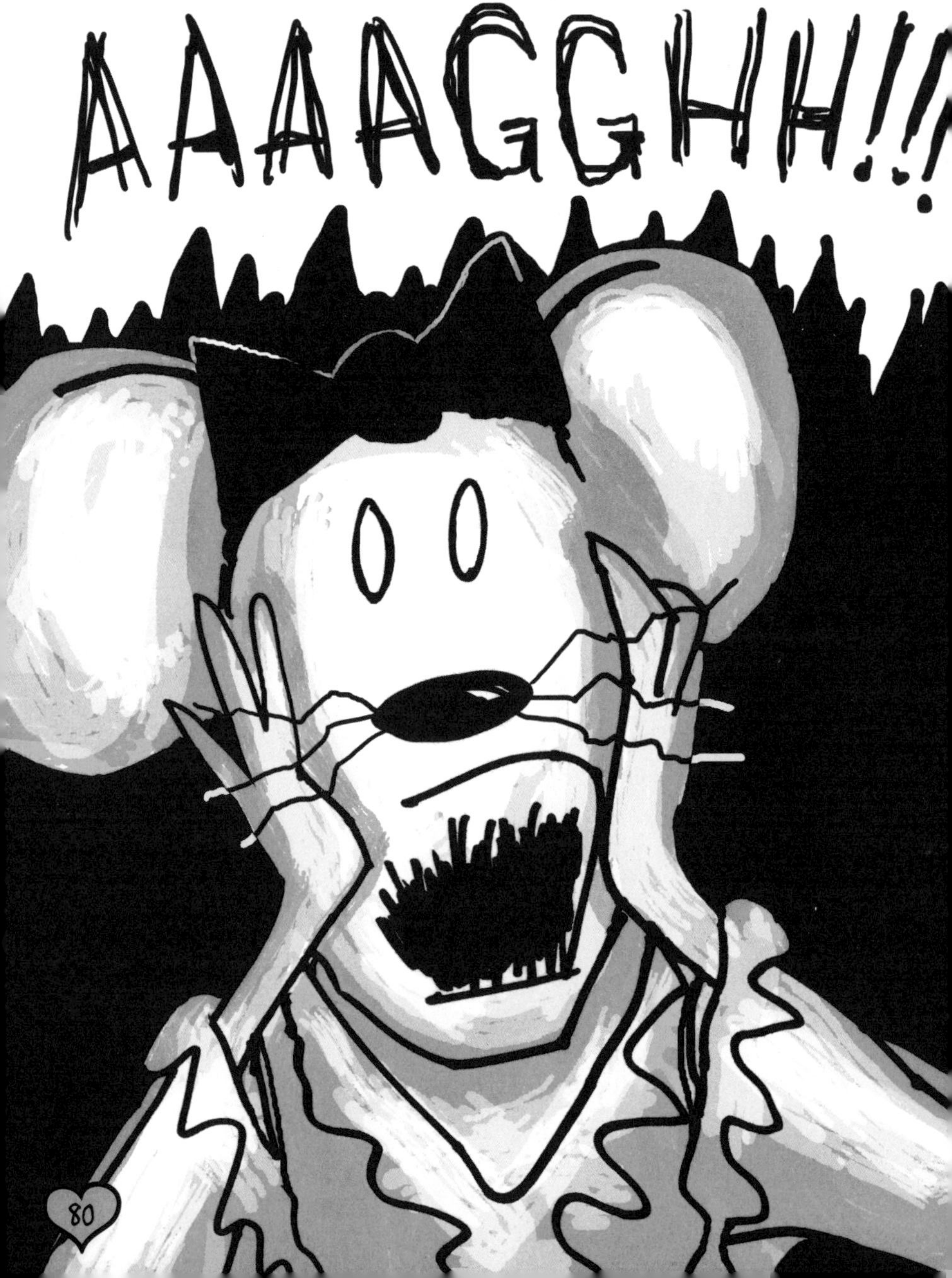
AAAAGGHH!!!

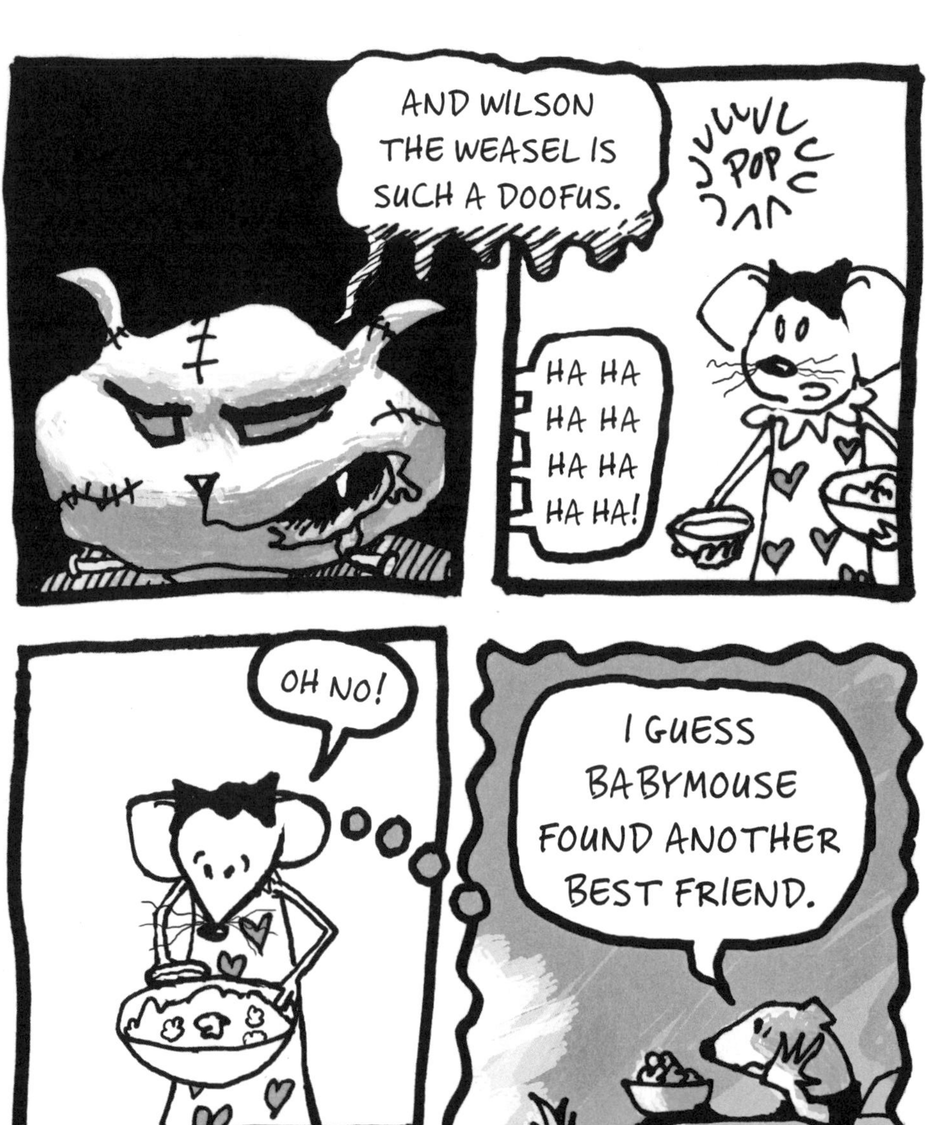
AND WILSON THE WEASEL IS SUCH A DOOFUS.
POP
HA HA HA HA HA HA HA HA!
OH NO!
WHAT HAD SHE DONE?
I GUESS BABYMOUSE FOUND ANOTHER BEST FRIEND.

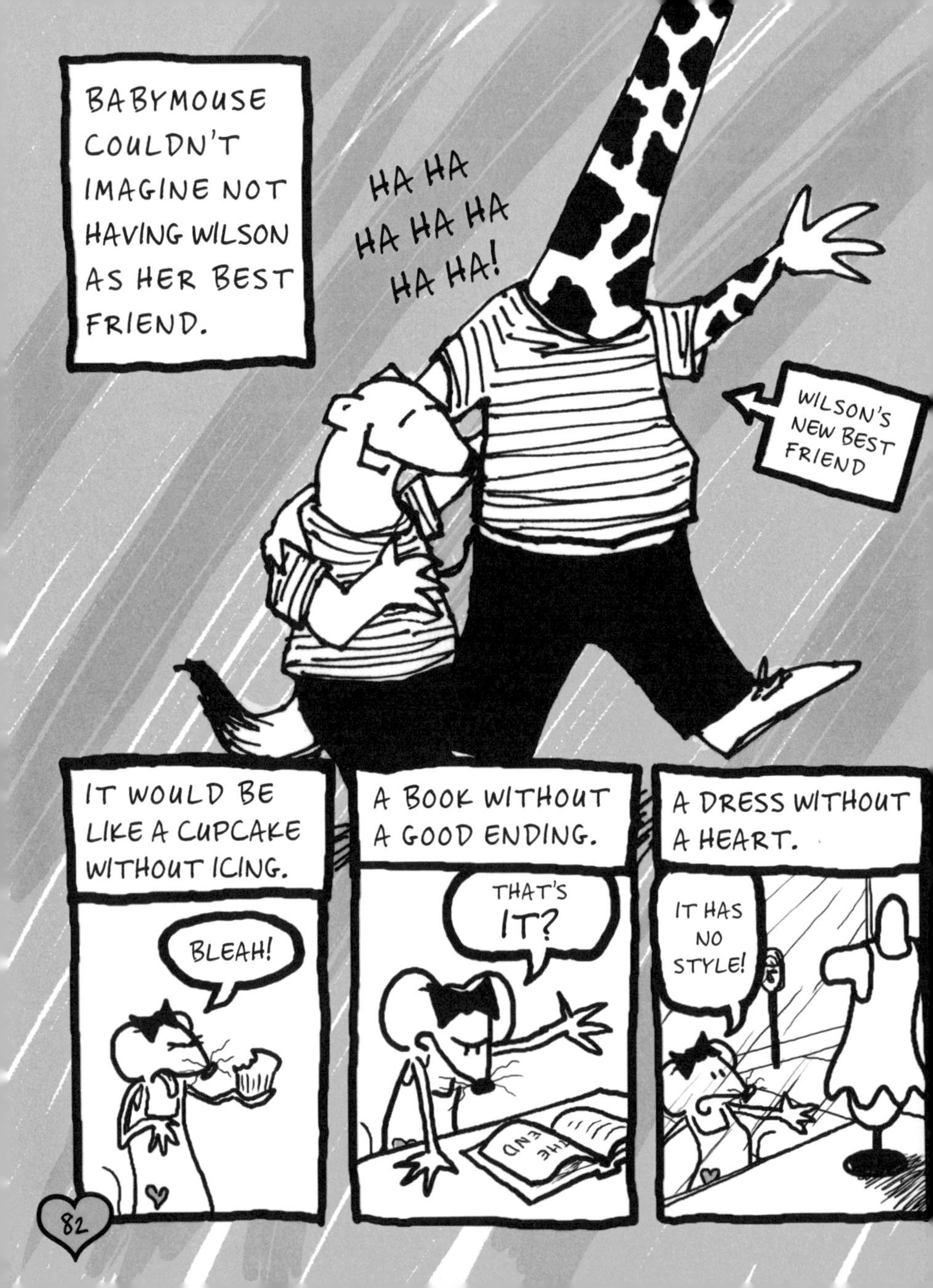
BABYMOUSE COULDN'T IMAGINE NOT HAVING WILSON AS HER BEST FRIEND.
HA HA HA HA HA HA HA!
WILSON'S NEW BEST FRIEND
IT WOULD BE LIKE A CUPCAKE WITHOUT ICING.
BLEAH!
A BOOK WITHOUT A GOOD ENDING.
THAT'S IT?
THE END
A DRESS WITHOUT A HEART.
IT HAS NO STYLE!

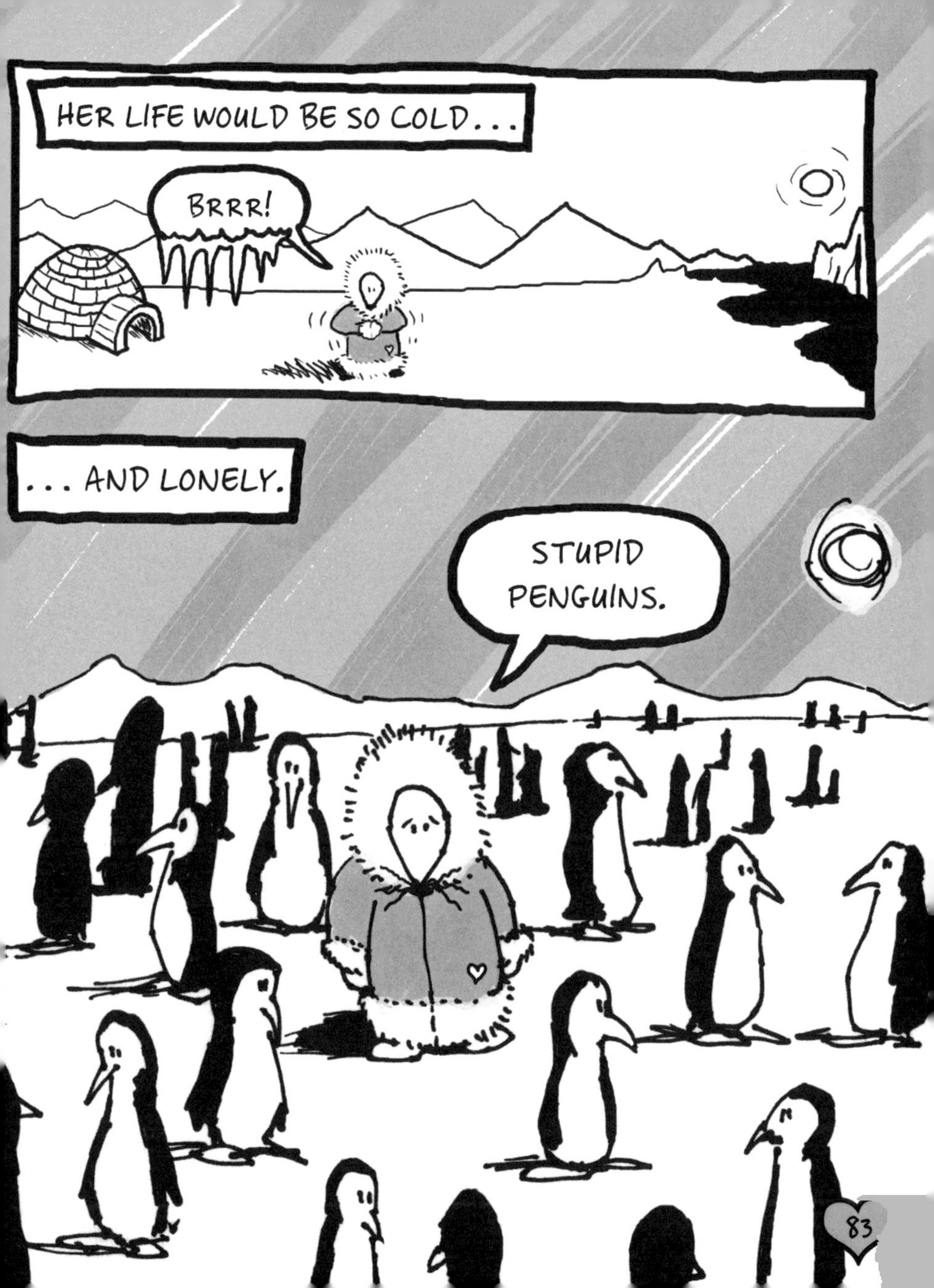
HER LIFE WOULD BE SO COLD...
BRRR!
...AND LONELY.
STUPID PENGUINS.
83

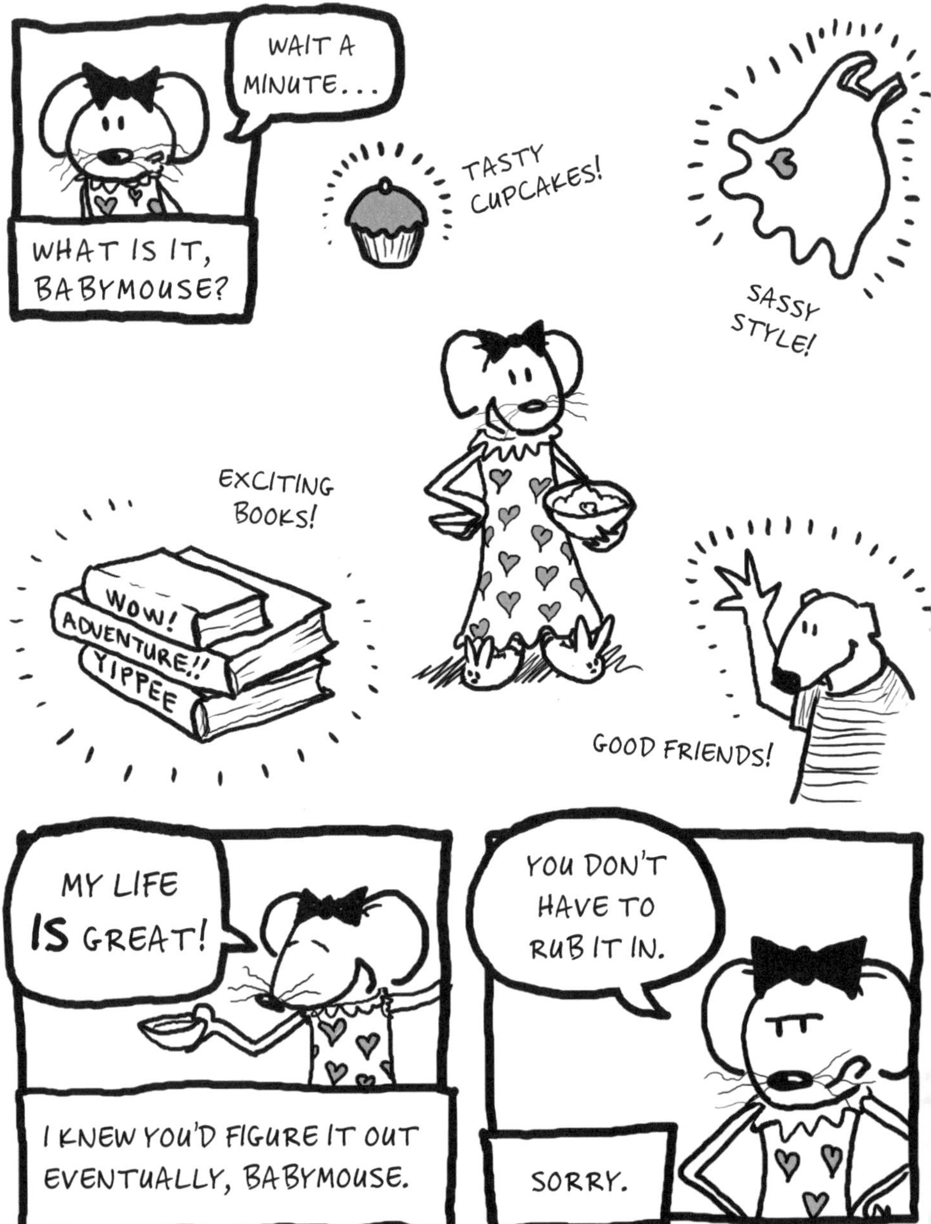
WAIT A MINUTE...
WHAT IS IT, BABYMOUSE?
TASTY CUPCAKES!
SASSY STYLE!
EXCITING BOOKS!
WOW!
ADVENTURE!!
YIPPEE
GOOD FRIENDS!
MY LIFE **IS** GREAT!
I KNEW YOU'D FIGURE IT OUT EVENTUALLY, BABYMOUSE.
YOU DON'T HAVE TO RUB IT IN.
SORRY.

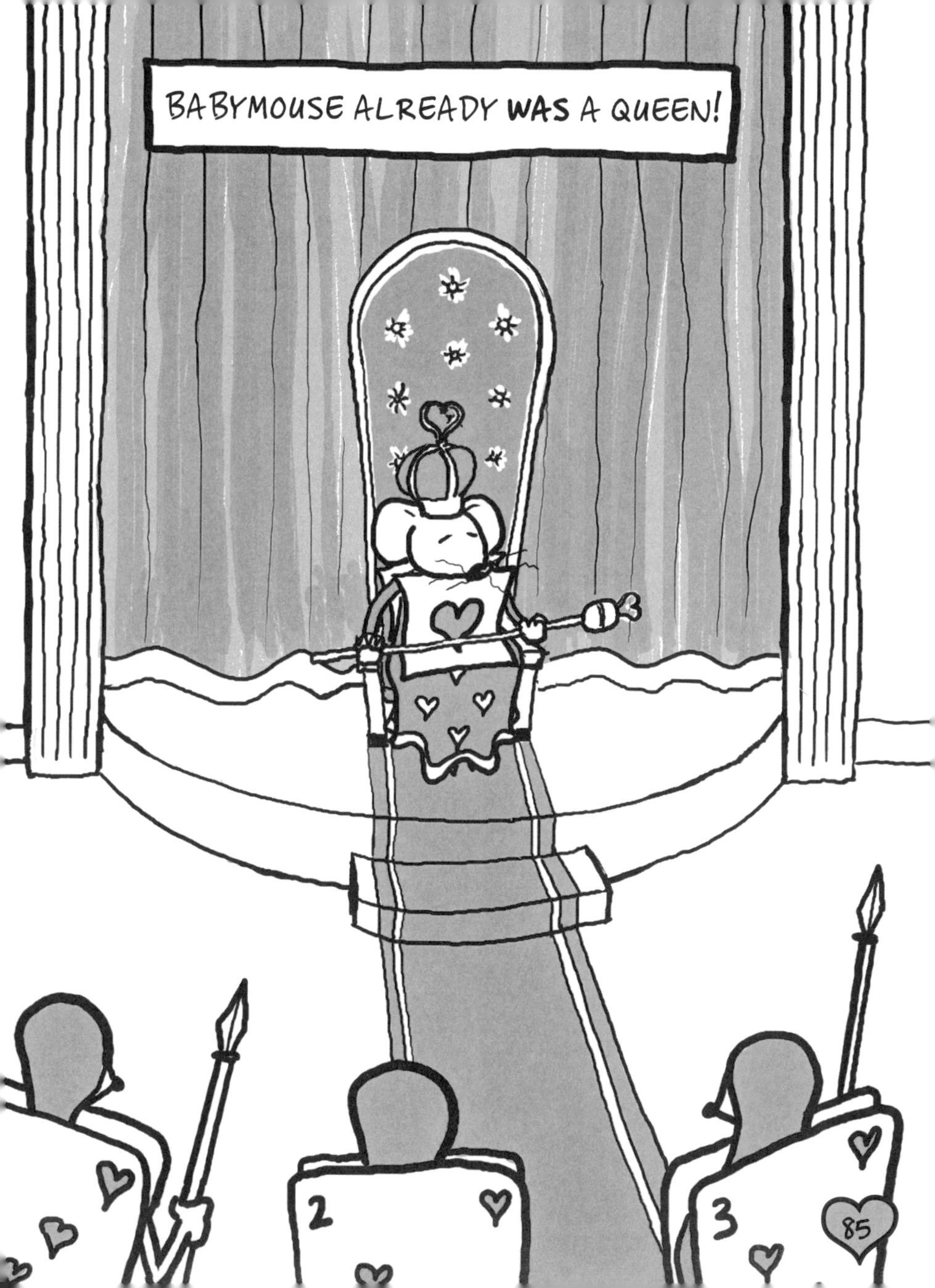
BABYMOUSE ALREADY WAS A QUEEN!
2
3

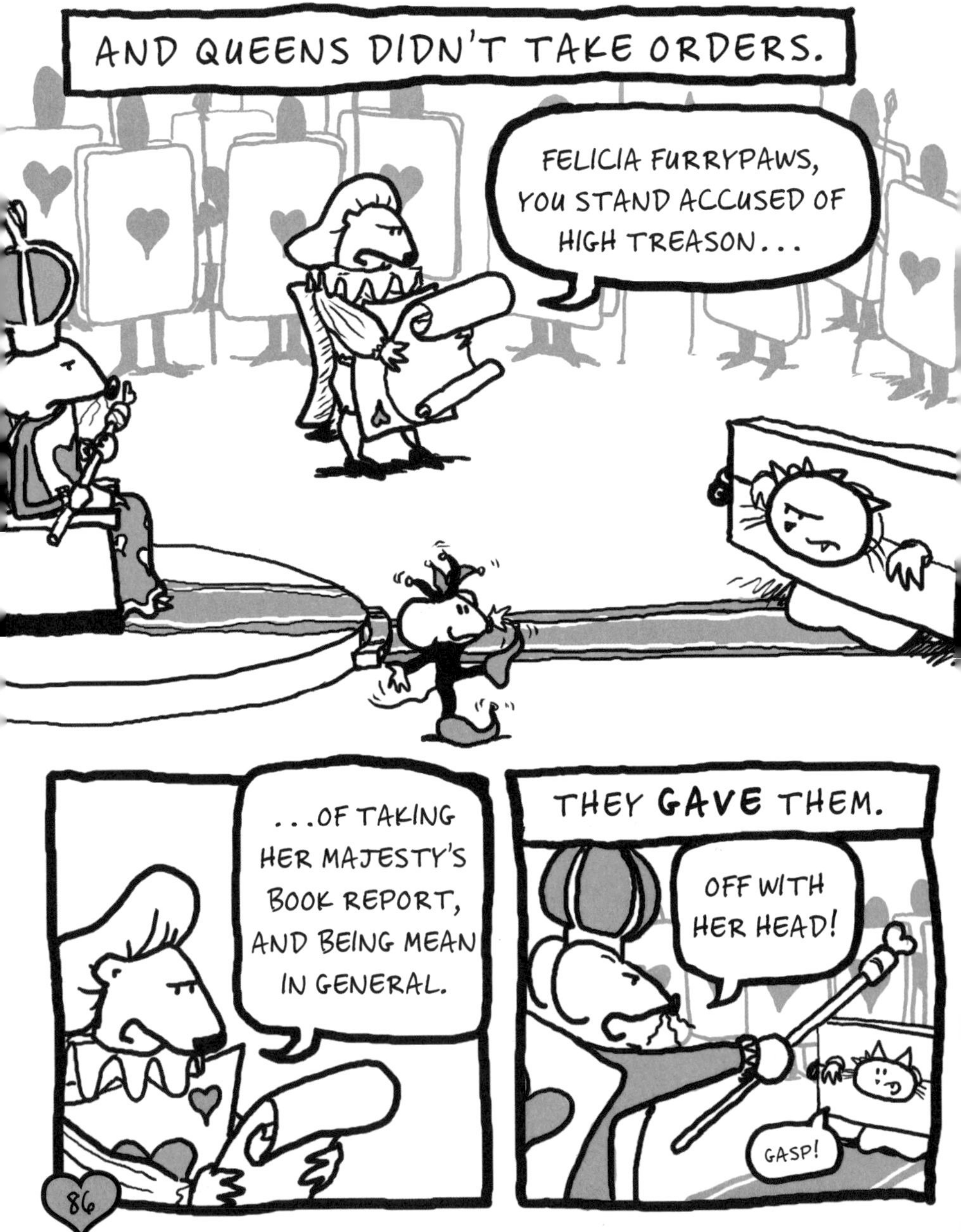
AND QUEENS DIDN'T TAKE ORDERS.
FELICIA FURRYPAWS, YOU STAND ACCUSED OF HIGH TREASON...
...OF TAKING HER MAJESTY'S BOOK REPORT, AND BEING MEAN IN GENERAL.
THEY **GAVE** THEM.
OFF WITH HER HEAD!
GASP!

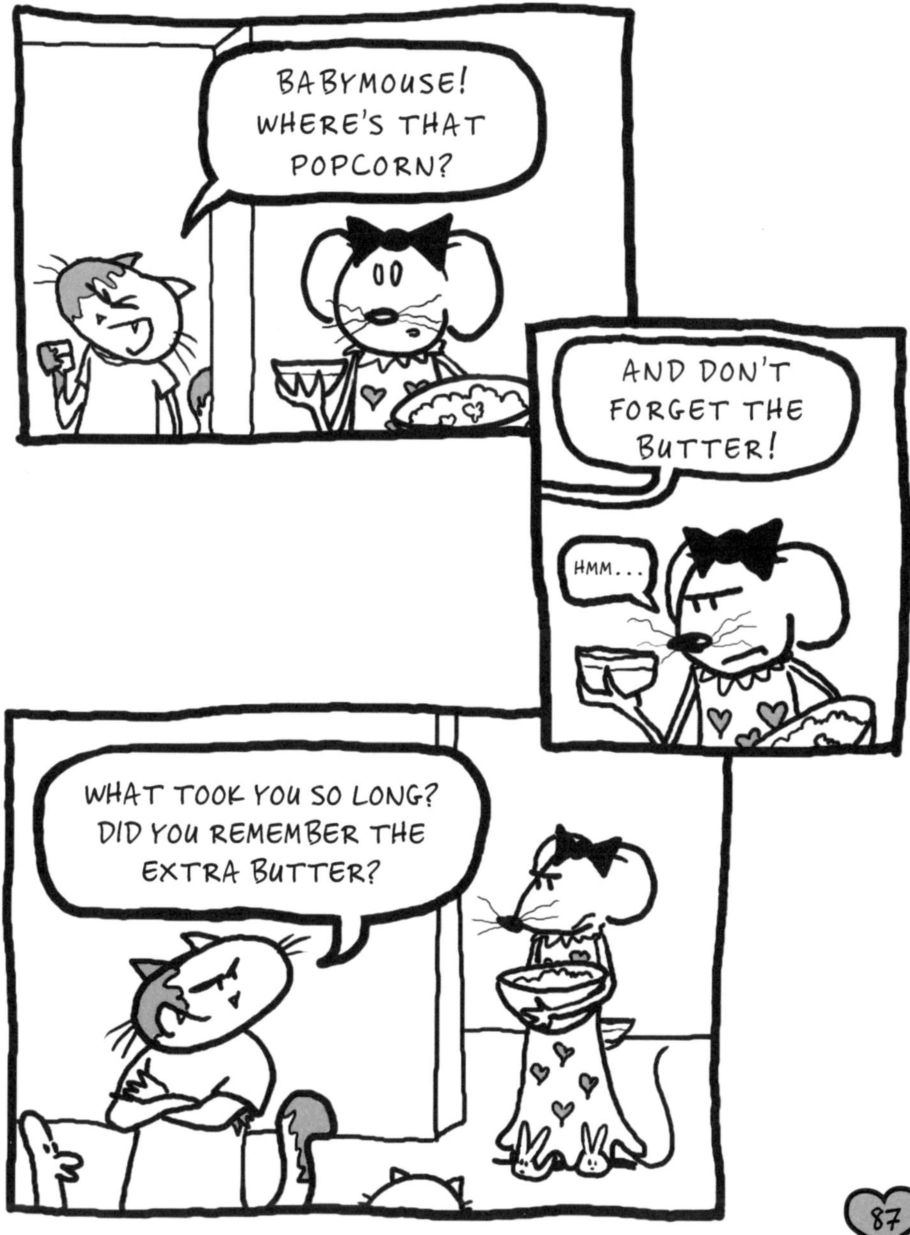
BABYMOUSE! WHERE'S THAT POPCORN?
AND DON'T FORGET THE BUTTER!
HMM...
WHAT TOOK YOU SO LONG? DID YOU REMEMBER THE EXTRA BUTTER?

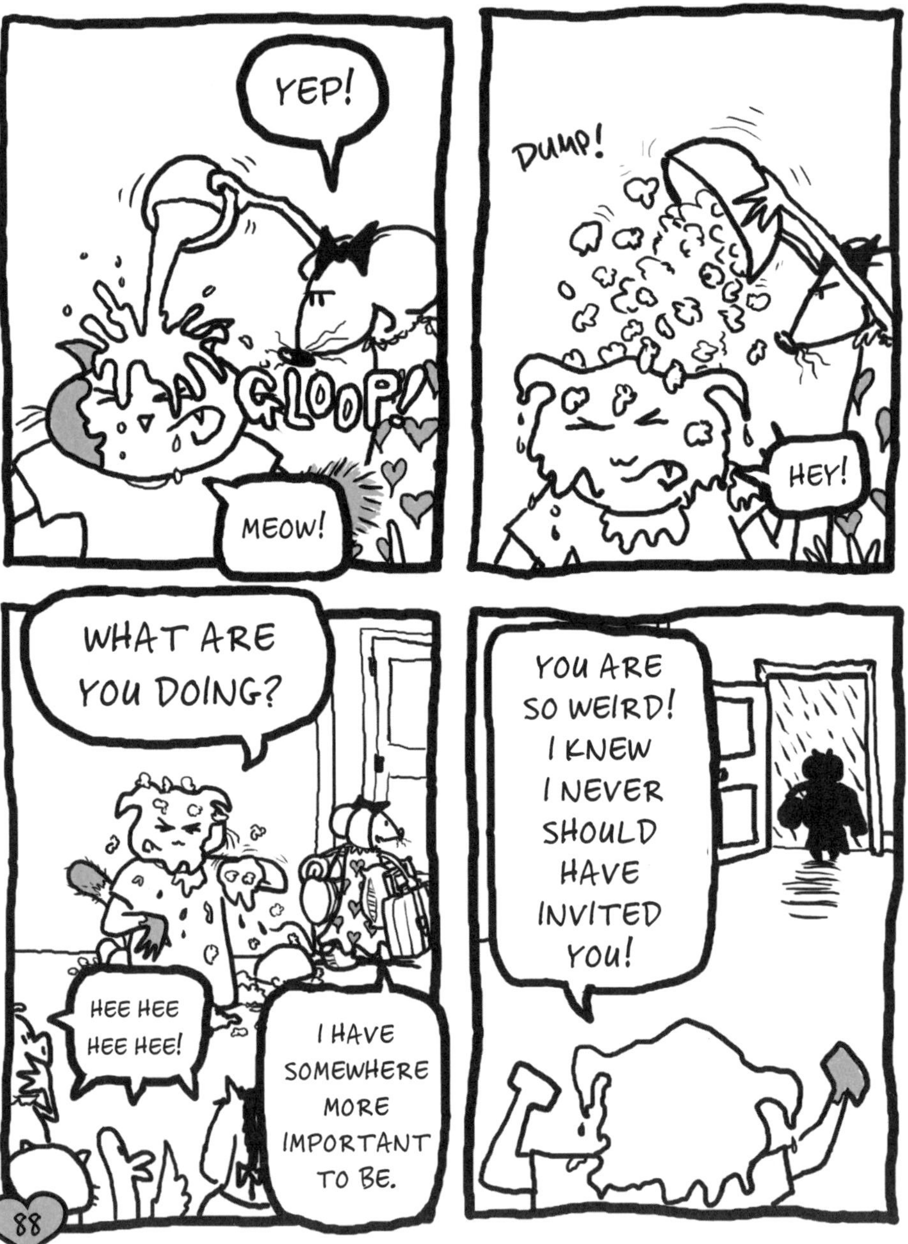
YEP!
GLOOP!
MEOW!
DUMP!
HEY!
WHAT ARE YOU DOING?
HEE HEE HEE HEE!
I HAVE SOMEWHERE MORE IMPORTANT TO BE.
YOU ARE SO WEIRD! I KNEW I NEVER SHOULD HAVE INVITED YOU!

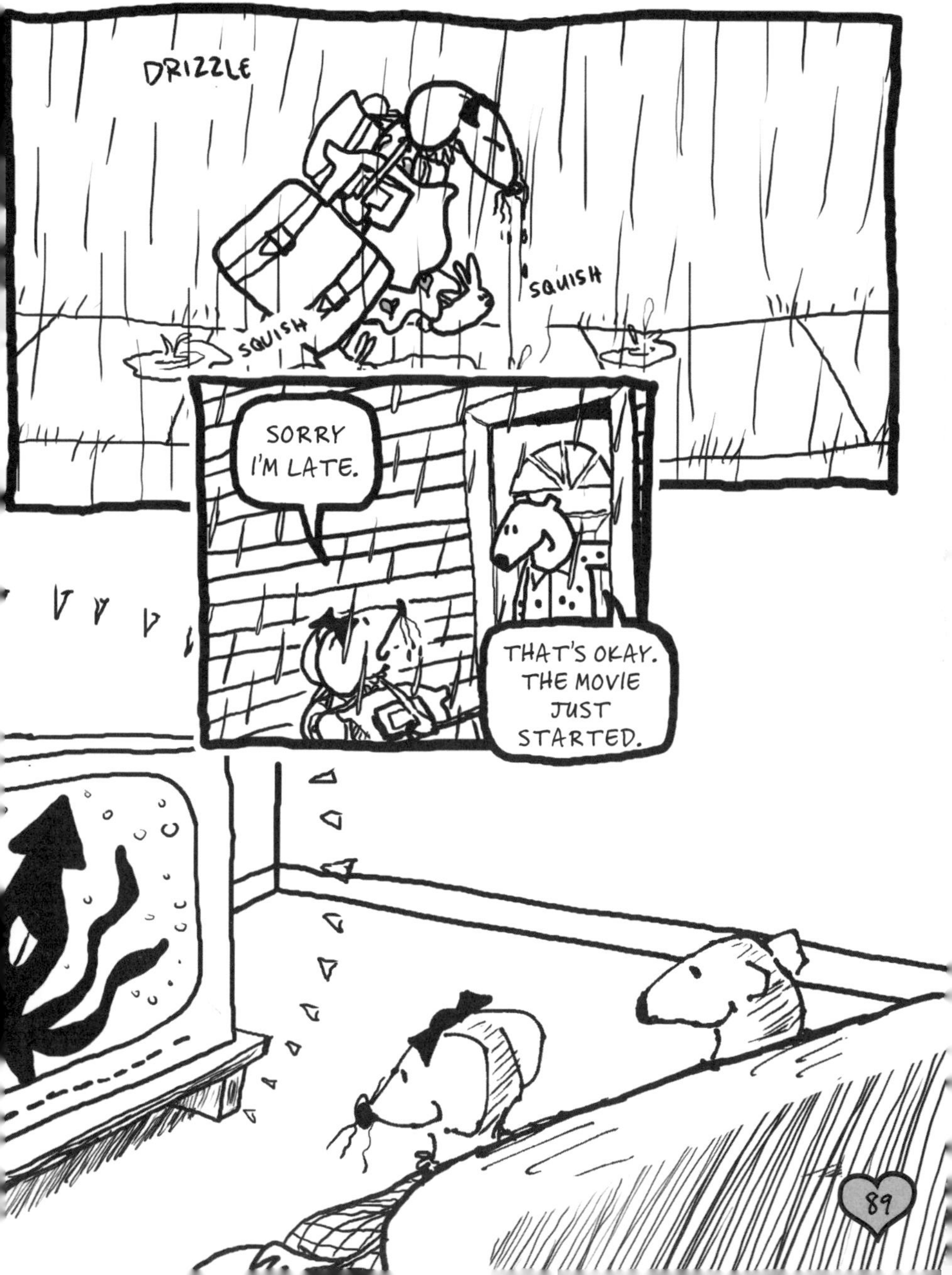
DRIZZLE
SQUISH
SQUISH
SORRY I'M LATE.
THAT'S OKAY. THE MOVIE JUST STARTED.

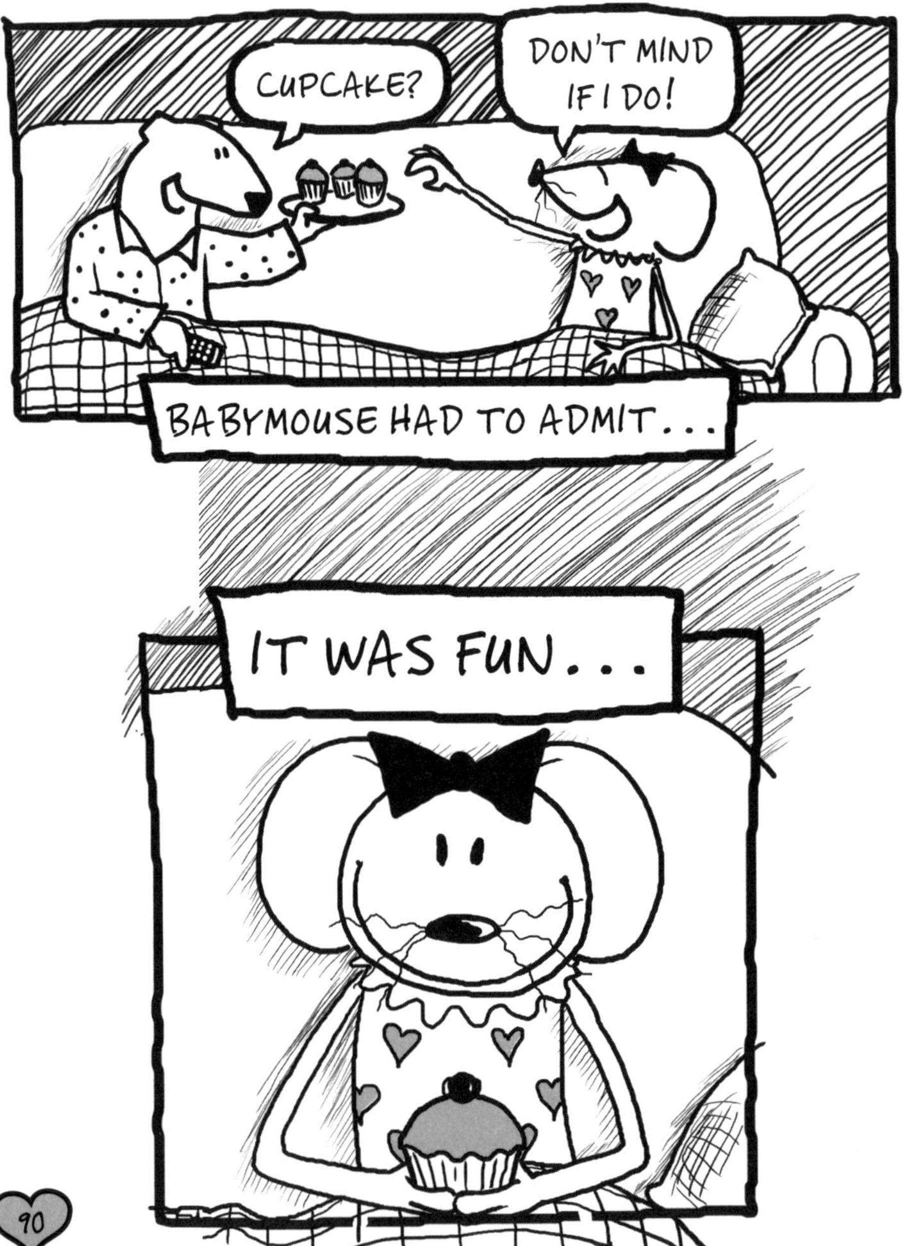
CUPCAKE?
DON'T MIND IF I DO!
BABYMOUSE HAD TO ADMIT...
IT WAS FUN...

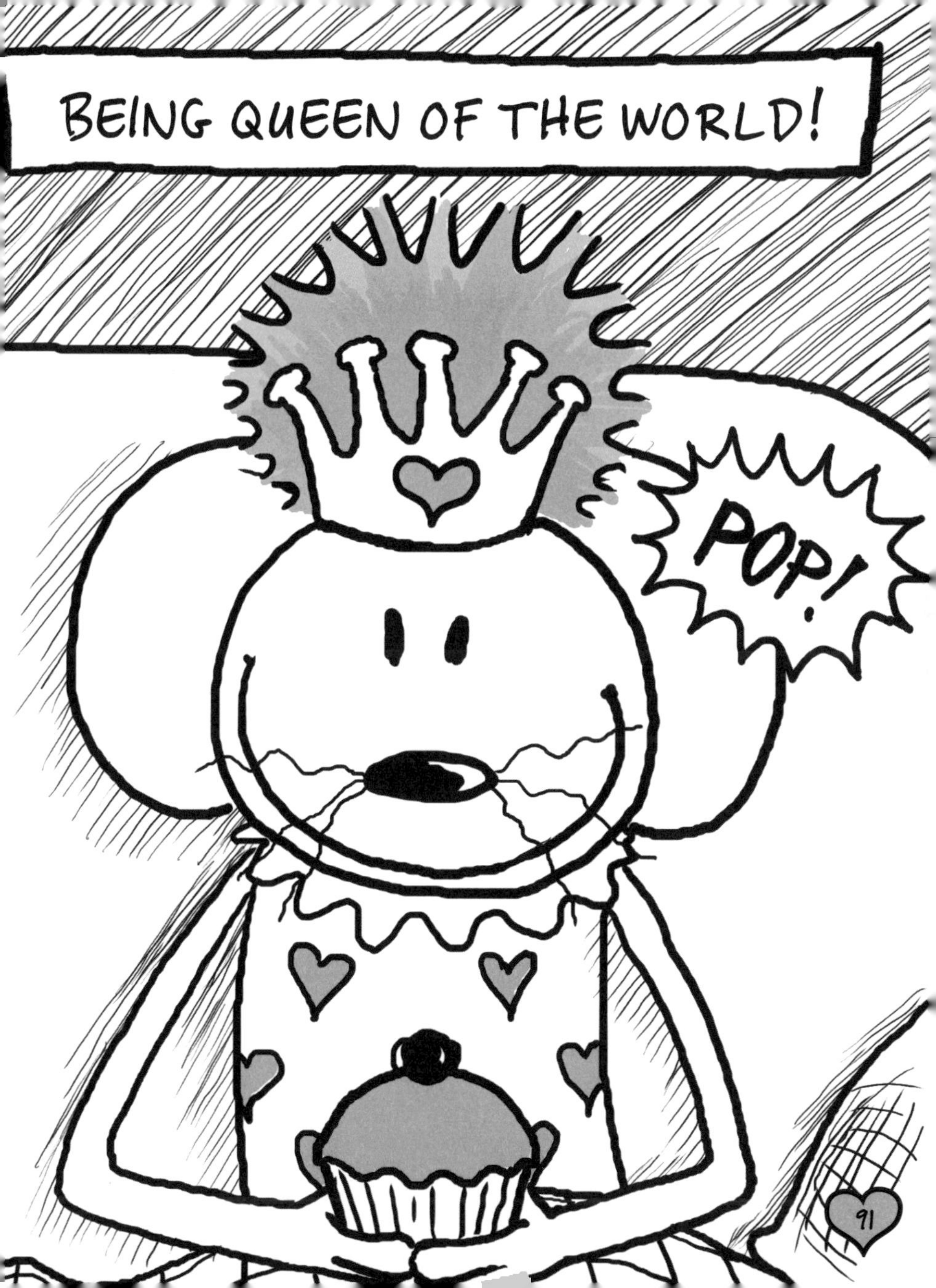
BEING QUEEN OF THE WORLD!
POP!

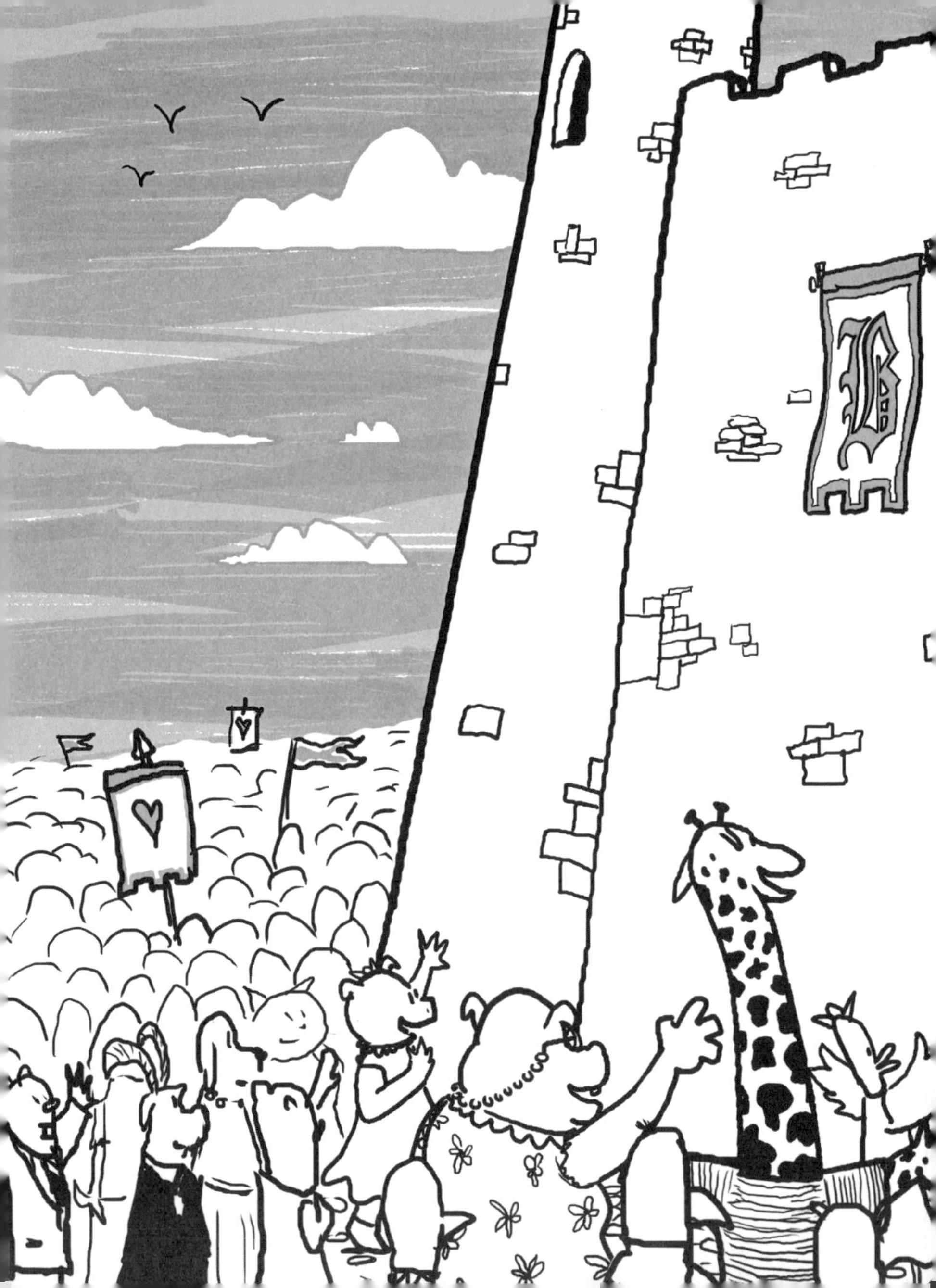
B

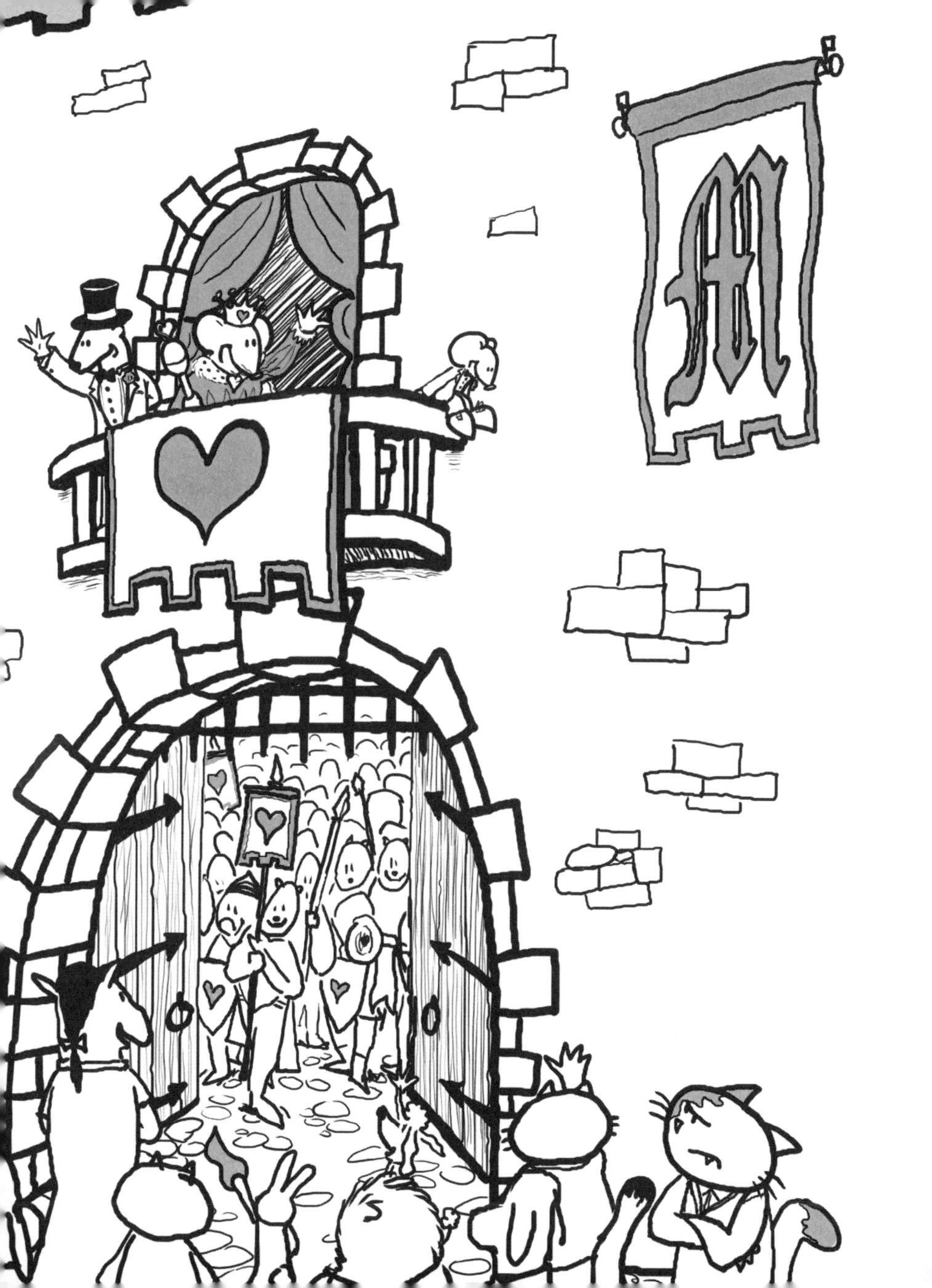

BABYMOUSE BONUS!

•LEARN HOW TO DRAW BABYMOUSE•

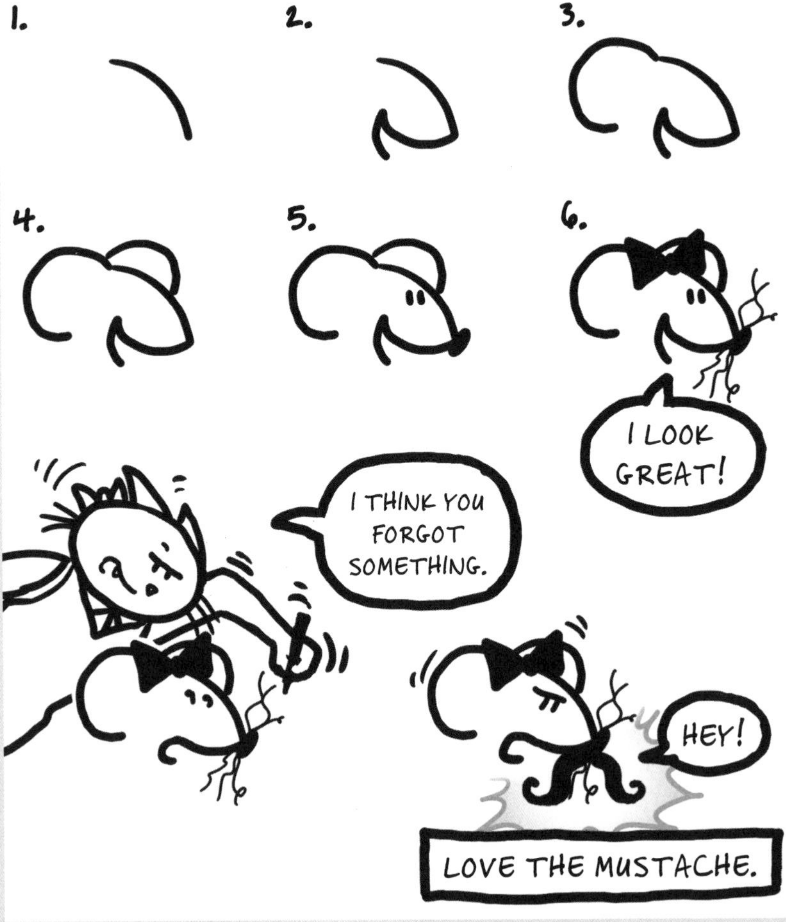
1.
2.
3.
4.
5.
6.
I LOOK GREAT!
I THINK YOU FORGOT SOMETHING.
HEY!
LOVE THE MUSTACHE.

BABYMOUSE BONUS!

•NOW YOU CAN MAKE YOUR OWN STORY•

Take that!
GLOOP!
Cheese sauce?
DUMP!
And popcorn?
Cheese sauce doesn't go with popcorn. It goes with nachos.
We love nachos!
The store was out of nachos. Sorry.
Next time you dump cheese sauce on my head, make sure you have nachos. And sour cream! And jalapeños!

GO TO BABYMOUSE.COM TO PRINT YOUR OWN COMIC TO FILL IN!

WATCH OUT, MIDDLE SCHOOL! HERE COMES BABYMOUSE.

SHE'S OLDER! MORE SOPHISTICATED! HER WHISKERS ARE **STILL** A MESS.

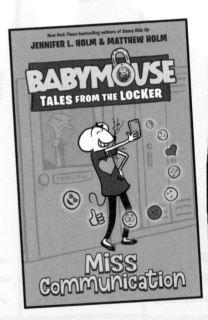

NEW SERIES AVAILABLE NOW!